LIFE

IN

PARALLEL

UNIVERSES

A Novel

by John E. Smethers, PhD

Life in Parallel Universes

ISBN-13: 978-1-906628-82-6
Published by CheckPoint Press, Ireland

CheckPoint
Press

www.checkpointpress.com

This book is dedicated
to my granddaughter

Kayla Castenada

Contents

CHAPTER ONE

Ed

When Bobby Hickman left Ed Smith's house, he felt tired but still not ready to go to bed, so he decided to take a ride in the desert to do some thinking. As he drove out on old Highway 247 toward Big Bear Lake from their home town of Barstow, California, he rolled down the window—the humidity was up, which rarely happens in the dry climate of the Mojave desert. He reached over to roll down the passenger-side window, and in doing so he took his eyes off the road momentarily; when he returned to his position, he saw nothing but two bright lights ahead of him, and then the crash—the shattering of glass, the screaming silence, and then darkness. He felt no pain, no knowledge of his surroundings, and no near-death experiences like leaving his body or a light at the end of a tunnel. His only observation was that of nothingness, and that he was no longer in the world as he previously knew it.

* * * *

A phone rings: "Hello."

"Hi, is this Mrs. Smith?

"Yes."

"I'm W.R. Hickman, and…"

"Oh, Bobby's brother. I don't think I've ever talked to you before."

"No, I don't believe you have," said W.R. as he squirmed around in his chair, "and I wish I didn't have to make this call, but first I'd like to know if Ed is home."

"Not at the moment. Is there something wrong?"

"Yes ma'am, I'm calling to let Ed know that Bobby was killed last night in an accident. His car got hit by a semi."

"OH MY GOD!" said Mrs. Smith as the color faded from her face. "I'm so sorry. You must be devastated."

* * * *

(The previous evening):

"Look, all you have to do is be at the wrong place at the wrong time," Bobby said as he snuffed out a smoldering Lucky Strike.

"The same goes for you. On your way home tonight you could get squashed by a semi-truck," replied Ed.

"That could happen to anyone."

Ed raised to a sitting position and looked at Bobby on the bed across from him and said, "I'm not saying that something *is* going to happen to you. All I'm saying is that you should be prepared in case it does."

In response Bobby said, "And how should I do that, Mr. Responsible?"

"Well, in the event that you get squashed by a semi on your way home tonight, why don't you write me out a will for your car?"

"Yeah, right."

That October night in 1964 they sat around arguing, talking about old times, drinking Brew 102, and listening to their favorite album, "The Paragons Meet the Jesters." It was getting late, so Bobby got up and said, "I've gotta go man, I have to work in the morning."

As Ed walked Bobby to the door he asked, "Will you pick me up tomorrow when you get off work? I get real bored around here when I'm not working."

"Okay, see ya 'bout three."

When Ed closed the door, he went to the front window and watched Bobby drive away in his black lowered 55 Studebaker Coupe. *What a neat car*, Ed thought as he watched him drive away.

* * * *

Since Mr. Smith was a day sleeper, he and his wife kept separate bedrooms. After the phone call from W.R., Ed's mother went to her bedroom, sat on her bed and cried, dreading what she had to do. She had no idea how her son was going to react to Bobby's death. Her thoughts went to Bobby, and she realized that he'd just turned 19—so young and full of life, and with such a wonderful personality. She recalled when her Eddy and Bobby first became friends in Jr. high school in 1956. She recalled a particular Sunday night when Bobby spent the night. It was the same night Elvis Presley made his nation wide T.V. appearance on the Ed Sullivan show—only being viewed from the waist up because of his supposedly vulgar gyrations.

Ed and Bobby graduated from high school in June of 1962. Now it was the fall of 1964, the leaves were beginning to give the trees that brown and barren look. October was an ideal time of year in Barstow—not too cold, yet not too warm.

For a graduation present Ed's father had their garage converted into a bedroom for Ed; however, it was still accessible from the main body of the house.

Ed woke up with a hangover and his mouth tasted bad from the previous night's brew. He put on his clothes, then rubbed his throbbing head on the way to the living room. Once he took some aspirin and finished his bowl of Cheerios, his headache subsided. He placed the bowl in the sink and went to the telephone to call Bobby at work.

"Morning, Denny's Restaurant."

"Morning to you too, any chance of talking to your cook, Bobby?"

"Bobby didn't come in today. Our graveyard cook is having to pull a double because of it."

"Oh. Well, I'll see if I can find him. Do you want him to call in?"

"Yes, but he still may be out of a job."

As Ed hung up the phone, he wondered why Bobby hadn't shown up for work. *This wasn't like him; especially since he had every intention of going to work,* Ed thought.

Just as he was hanging up the phone, his short, fair-haired mother entered the room with her crooked hanging apron and asked, "Who were you talking to, honey?" Her face full of concern.

"Bobby's job," replied Ed, displaying a puzzled look. "He didn't show up for work this morning."

Evelyn then realized that it was time to break the awful news to her son. "Eddy." She said.

"Yeah."

"I have something to tell you."

Ed looked at her curiously and replied, "What?"

First she closed her eyes and said a quick prayer: *"Dear God, please give me the strength to deliver this message, and give him the strength to endure it. Amen."*

"Sit down baby, I have bad news. Uh . . . Bobby's brother called . . . and . . . uh . . ., he called for you, but . . . but decided that I could give you the message."

Ed replied with an ominous, "Well?"

"Honey . . . Uh . . . Well . . ., Bobby was involved in a car accident last night."

10

Ed was silent, then with a shocked expression, he asked, "And?"

The distraught woman bowed her head. Before she could answer him, he asked, "How bad Mom?"

Again she bowed her head. When she raised it again, she didn't have to say a word, because there were tears on her cheeks, and she could tell by his expression that her tears said it all.

He didn't utter a word. He just sat there staring at nothing. Finally, when his expression relaxed a little, he asked, "How did it happen?"

"A collision with a semi-truck." She replied, trying to regain her self-composure and wiping the tears away with the palms of her hands.

Suddenly he looked as if he just learned the news again. Again he displayed a shocked expression. The concerned mother felt compelled to come to her son's emotional rescue, "His death was instant, baby——he didn't have to suffer."

That was no consolation, because he felt like he was somehow responsible for the accident with the semi-truck.

"Eddy?" She said, just wanting to ease his pain any way she could.

Ed just looked at her in silence.

When his expression started to relax again and the color started returning to his face, she consoled him. "Honey, I *do* know how you feel. When my mother died I felt a lot like you do right now. She was my mother. You were only nine years old at the time–too young to really understand the meaning of death. I didn't allow you to see my suffering. Whether that was wrong or right, I don't know. The only person that I could turn to was my husband. Your daddy comforted me and helped me through it. If you would like to talk about it, I'm always here. If not, I'm still here for you. Honey, you're my only son, the only child I've

11

ever had or will have, and your daddy feels the same way. He loves you very much. You're more important to us than anything in the world. We love you very much, and I know this isn't going to be easy for you. We loved Bobby too."

"Thanks Mom, but I'll be okay," Ed replied as he stood up. "Right now all I want to do is go to my room."

"Okay Baby. Can I get you anything? Are you hungry? Could I make you some Kool-Aid?"

"No thanks." On his way back to his side of the house, he changed his mind and went back, "On second thought, Mom, would you mind going down and buying me a couple of six-packs of Coors?"

Being against it, but at the same time relieved that she could at least do something, she agreed. "Okay honey, at a time like this maybe that would be the best medicine. I'll be right back."

As Ed's worried mother exited the front door, Ed went back to the security of his room.

The shock of hearing about Bobby's death was bad enough, but coupled with the previous night's conversation about the semi-truck, Ed was left in horrified silence as he sat on his bed and waited for his mother's return.

* * * *

Ed, Bobby, and their friends, Huck and Jimbo had been drinking and doing drugs for a couple years. These four young men had been friends since junior high school days. Many of their cohorts referred to them as *the big four*.

There wasn't much for young people to do in Barstow. The big four kept their drug use as obscure as possible, but they made no secret of their drinking habits. In 1964, drug use in Barstow was a social stigma.

About a month later, after Ed helped Bobby's family with

funeral arrangements such as picking the pall bearers and sending out thank-you cards to the people that provided flowers, he was visiting Bobby's girlfriend at her parent's house.

Ed and Shirlee were in her bedroom playing records and talking one evening. As they reminisced, Ed asked, "You and Bobby had been going together for about a year, right?"

"Yes," She replied, "But it was on shaky ground. He'd rather be out with you guys getting drunk than be with me. Other than that we got along okay, I guess."

"So you were probably as upset with me and our other friends as you were with him, huh?"

"Not really. Guys will be guys, but if a guy is supposed to be in love, he should show it, and it isn't showing it when he's always out drinking with his friends."

"Yeah, you're right."

Ed and Shirlee talked for about an hour when there was a light tap on the door. Shirlee knew who it was and answered, "Come on in, Mom."

Shirlee's mother stuck her head in and said, "Hi Ed, how've you been?"

"Oh, pretty good I guess, and you?"

"Just fine, thank you," she replied, then turned to her daughter and said, "This is Sunday, Shirlee, you have chores and homework to do, you know."

"I know Mom, but this is the first time I've talked to Ed since Bobby died. They were best friends, you know."

When Shirlee's mother answered, she was looking at Ed. "I'm worried about my daughter, Ed. I'm not trying to hurry you or be rude, but since Bobby died, Shirlee hasn't been herself. Death takes its toll on the living too," Shirlee's mother explained sympathetically, "But life goes on." Then she left the room.

Ed was raised with the old belief that men don't cry;

however, as the strained conversation progressed about their mutual friend, it led to both of them breaking down.

Up to this point in Ed's life, he had no idea what grief was—he'd never felt it before. He really didn't know how to deal with such a tragedy in his life. His normally affable, easygoing, good-natured and fun-loving personality had suddenly changed into an edgy, snappy, and very moody one—leaving him often withdrawn and melancholy.

Ed's emotional despair had dissipated some by the first of the year of 1965, which was about four months after Bobby's death. One night, Ed was out drinking beer and smoking pot with his friends, Huck and Jimbo. They always went to isolated spots in the desert to avoid being caught by the police.

Tonight, the discussion was all about Bobby's death and Ed was the last one that Huck took home. Having a fairly good buzz on, Ed went to his part of the house by the side entrance and went directly to his hi-fi set, put on a random stack of forty-fives, then hit the select button. Ed had been collecting records since grammar school; the first of which were 78's, before 45's came out. The first record that dropped onto the turntable and began playing was *Peggy Sue* by Buddy Holly. Buddy Holly had been killed, and that reminded Ed of his friend. He immediately rejected it and removed the stack of 45's so the hi-fi set would turn itself off.

It was then that he heard a voice in his mind, but it wasn't very clear. It was Bobby's voice! He immediately dismissed it, attributing it to the booze and pot. His recent indulgence in pot-smoking wasn't as rewarding as it was before Bobby's death. Evidently, the pot made him think of Bobby's death more, keeping him from enjoying the high. As a result he leaned more heavily on alcohol.

Suddenly Ed felt another sensitivity created by the pot—hunger. It was after midnight, and his father was working on his patrol. Mr. Smith was the owner of Barstow Merchant's Patrol, which he operated himself along with two hired patrolmen. Ed figured if he was quiet, he could go into the kitchen and fix himself something to eat without waking his mother.

As he sat eating his bologna and cheese sandwich, he heard Bobby's familiar voice again, but like the last time, he couldn't really hear it very good. A chill came over him. He finished his sandwich and milk, then left to go back to the security of his room. As he entered, he grabbed the stack of 45's and put them back onto the turntable and hit 'select'. Of all the records, it was the one by Jody Reynolds entitled *Endless Sleep*. Again he rejected it, thinking about his friend's endless sleep. When the next record dropped, Paul Anka started singing *Lonely Boy*. That was all he could take. He turned off the machine and decided to go for a walk to clear his head. He assumed that the pot and beer were responsible for his apparent delusions.

Finally he was snapping out of the euphoria induced by the pot and alcohol as he breathed the crisp fresh desert air. As his mind began to clear, he thought about the eerie experience of hearing Bobby's voice.

Ed lit a cigarette and sat on a short wall in front of a neighborhood house, trying to put his thoughts into some kind of order. By this time the effects of the pot and booze had pretty much worn off. He got up, flipped his cigarette butt into the street and headed back home to the comforting environment of his room.

Once he arrived, as a force of habit, he went directly to his hi-fi set, hesitated, then turned it on. He sat on his bed and waited for the next record to drop. Being apprehensive, he wondered what significance the next selection would have concerning what had been weighing so heavily on his mind. The needle dropped to the outer edge of the record. Suddenly he reached over and jerked the arm of the record player off the record that was about to play, pulled up the stack of forty-fives along with the spindle they rested on, switched the record speed from 45 to 33, then he grabbed one of his and Bobby's favorite albums and put it on: *The Paragons Meet the Jesters*. The first song that played was "Let's Start All Over Again." At that very instant Ed heard Bobby's voice again–this time as clearly as if he were sitting next to him. Bobby said, *"Ed, let's really do start all over again."*

When this occurred, Ed formed a mental image of his friend, which totally engulfed him. Unaware that the recent turn of events would be the turning point and the beginning of something so astoundingly miraculous that it would greatly affect, beyond his wildest imagination, the rest of his natural life, he figured he might as well go along with what was happening.

Ed wasn't really familiar with meditation per se, but he was meditating. When he finally came out of his reverie, he made a subliminal connection with Bobby and the evening's turn of events: the eerie and unfamiliar feeling of fear, the implications of the records that played, his friend's voice, and their mutually favorite song on the album, "Let's Start All Over Again." This set the stage for him to hear Bobby's voice speaking to him— asking him the question that was also the title to their favorite song. This left no doubt in his mind that his dead friend was really trying to communicate with him.

* * * *

"Hello."

"Hey, what are you up to?" Ed asked into the telephone.

Huck recognized his friend's voice and answered, "I just got finished putting a water pump on my mom's car. Why? What are you doing?"

"Oh, nothin'. Just wanted to know if you wanted to drink some beer?"

"You got money?"

"Yeah, and you have a car so why don't you come and get

16

me?"

"All right," replied Huck as he too straightened the telephone cord, "But first I have to take a shower."

"Okay, see you when you get here."

Just as Ed was hanging up the phone, his mother walked in the front door from work and asked, "Who were you talking to baby?"

"Huck," Ed replied. "He's coming over to pick me up so we can go look for work."

"That's a good idea, honey. All you boys should be working. It'll help take your minds off that terrible accident with Bobby."

"I don't want to talk about it."

"Well, it doesn't do any good to keep it all bottled up.."

"He's dead, Mom. Let him rest in peace. Talking about dead people doesn't do any good. Life goes on."

"The problem is, honey, you may not want to talk about it, but you're sure doing a lot of thinking about it. You haven't really been the same since it happened. I'm worried about you."

"That's nice, Mom, but I'll be fine. Right now I've got to get dressed to go look for work." Ed really just wanted to get away from her motherly nagging, and get back to the privacy of his room until Huck arrived.

It had been over a month since the night Ed heard Bobby's voice. As time heals all wounds, time was also lessening the impact of his grief. Of course if his parents knew what he was really experiencing, they would've had something to worry about. If he had mentioned hearing voices to either of them, they would've thought he was going off the deep end. However, for a while, he thought the same thing himself. Ed was emotionally stable and quite confident of his sanity. He knew what he knew, at least he thought he did, and he didn't see or hear things that weren't there, or at least he thought he didn't. He decided he wouldn't let anybody know his secret. He knew what had happened, really did happen, but even though it hadn't happened since, it didn't eliminate the reality of it.

Ed looked out of his bedroom window and saw Huck pull up in his old Chevy. As his mother watched her son out of the living room window, Ed got into Huck's car and they sped away.

It was the first part of the windy month of March. The wind gets strong on the high desert around this time of year. On this particular day it was also cold.

Once in the car with Huck, Ed shivered and said, "Turn on the fucking heater, what's wrong with you?"

"The *fuckin* heater doesn't work."

"Why don't you fix it then?"

"Why don't you fix it for me?"

"You're the mechanic. Besides, it's your car."

"You're the one that's cold."

"Just go to the store okay, I'm thirsty." Ed said as he lit a cigarette.

"What store?"

"Farmer's Market, that's the only place they'll sell it to me."

"Why didn't you say so in the first place? Now I have to turn around and go back the other way."

"If your heater was working, I would have."

"Oh, another thing; I need gas," said Huck.

"Okay, I'll put some in. Want me to buy you a new heater, too?"

"Why that's mighty nice of you. Would you install it for me, too?"

"Yeah sure. Listen asshole, all I want to do is get drunk – so

18

that I can put up with you."

They pulled up to the market and Ed jumped out and entered the store.

Meanwhile, Huck turned on his radio and started looking for a radio station. Suddenly the Beatles were singing, *"I Want to Hold Your Hand,"* then just for the hell of it he reached over and switched on the heater. He thought to himself, *"I'll be damned! It must be an electrical problem."* Then he smiled. *"He's gonna be fit to be tied when he gets back."*

Ed opened the passenger door and sat the case of Brew 102 on the seat between them. Before he got in, he heard the heater's fan motor. He looked at the heater, then he looked at Huck with that, you son-of-a-bitch, look on his face.

"Well? Get in. What are you just standing there looking stupid for?" Then Huck started laughing.

When Ed got in and closed the door, Huck started the car and peeled out—tires screeching as they hit the pavement. He hit second gear and scratched again. Ed was still just sitting there staring at him blankly when Huck started slowing down, "What's wrong with you? Open me a beer, I'm thirsty. And don't start sniveling about it being cold in here, either. I felt sorry for you and fixed the heater."

Ed was still staring at him.

Then Huck added, "Now you don't have to buy me a heater," and he started laughing again.

* * * *

Ed's mom had good reason to be concerned. Her son had adopted more than just a passing interest in drugs and alcohol. She didn't bother mentioning it to his father. There was no sense in alarming him—just in case it was only temporary. She hoped he'd slow down, but now she began to wonder.

Evelyn waited up—worrying about Ed, as parents will. Of course she knew that Ed and Huck weren't out looking for work until after midnight. It was around twelve thirty when she heard Huck's car pull up and let her son out. She peered out of the window and watched him stagger toward the entrance on his side of the house.

When Ed entered his room, he immediately flopped down on his bed.

What happened next took him by surprise. As clear as if *Bobby* were in the room with him, he heard the voice of his friend in his mind.

"Ed? Like our song says, let's start all over again. We have to get reacquainted, ole buddy."

Ed was drunk, which was part of the reason Bobby would pick such times to get this started.

Without uttering a word, in his mind Ed replied, *"Okay Bobby, dead person, talk to me."*

"Wise Ass! You're drunk."

"I was drunk the last time you did this, too."

"Ed, I've had to approach this delicately and very gradual. I'm sure you can understand that."

"Why though?" Ed asked out loud, slurring his words.

"Why what?"

"Why this? Why me? Why you? Why is all this happening?"

"It happens to everybody, Ed, but through some act of nature, we're conscious of it, but first get some sleep. You've got a good buzz on right now. We can continue this conversation in the morning when your head is clearer."

"Okay Bobby, dead person, I am sleepy."

Ed was asleep by the time his head hit the pillow. When he awoke, he was suffering with a hangover, complete with a throbbing headache. He got up and went to his medicine cabinet and took three Anacin, then went to the living room where his mother was sitting.

"Hi Mom"

"You look awful, baby."

"With good reason—I feel awful, but if someone would fix me something to eat, maybe I'd start feeling a little better."

"Okay, go wash your face, and I'll call you when it's ready."

"Thanks Mom."

When Ed finished his breakfast he placed his dirty dishes in the sink and almost bumped into his dad.

"Hi, Bub," said Hank.

"Hi, Dad."

"Haven't seen much of you lately, Son. What have you been up to?"

"Not much Dad. Huck and I have been trying to find some work, but ever since Bobby died it's been hard to get motivated."

"You know what they say about Idle time." Hank warned as he sat in his chair and adjusted his reading glasses.

As Ed started back to his room he said, "Yeah I know, I'm working on it."

When Ed got back to his room, he felt better since he washed his face and had breakfast. He was still hung over, though. He laid back down on his bed, vaguely remembering the previous night's conversation. So, Bobby took that as a cue to continue the conversation. *"Have a hangover, ole buddy?"*

When Ed heard his friend's voice in his mind, he replied with his mind, as though he were thinking: *"As a matter of fact, I do, but that's beside the point. What I want to know is how I can be having a conversation with a dead person without opening my* mouth?"

"Like our favorite song says—let's start all over again. I could overdose you with all this right now, but I won't, so we're gonna have to take it easy. Okay?

"Yeah. I'm not in much of a position to argue with you."

"How are you with all this?" Bobby Asked.

"How would you feel? I don't know . . ., but I guess I'm relieved in a way, because in a way, you're not really dead."

"Well, the fact is, I'm not dead."

"Is that right? Then why did I see you in a coffin at your funeral?"

"Why don't you get adjusted to the fact that we're really communicating before I start explaining what's happening. Is that okay with you?

"Yeah, I guess," Ed replied.

"Do you think you can get comfortable with all this?"

"I think so. I'm not thinking about ending up in the funny farm or anything, if that's what you mean. I guess the shock is starting to wear off."

"Good. Then you understand why I've been taking so long and not too much at a time?"

"Yeah, I guess I do. You always were one to take advantage of a drunk, you asshole."

"Good," said Bobby, a little relieved. "I'm glad you called me asshole. I take that to mean you're getting used to me again. I just can't explain everything to you right now, Ed.

Ed lied back down on his bed, still a little confused, and after a while he went to sleep.

CHAPTER TWO

Bobby

When Ed Smith dropped off his friend, Bobby Hickman, at his parents' house, he wasn't tired and not quite ready to go home. It was a beautiful night, so Ed decided to take a ride in the desert in his low-rider 58 Chevy to do some thinking. As he drove out of their home town of Barstow, on old Highway 466 toward Bakersfield, he thought about how rocky his relationship with his girlfriend, Shirlee, had been lately. About ten miles out of town, he pulled over and parked on the shoulder. Since it was rather warm out, he started rolling down all the windows. When he returned to his position behind the wheel after rolling down the rear windows, he saw nothing but two bright lights ahead of him—and then the crash, the shattering of glass, the screaming silence, and then darkness. He had no pain, no knowledge of his surroundings, and no near-death experiences like leaving his body or a light at the end of a tunnel. His only observation was that of nothingness, and that he was no longer in the world as he previously knew it.

* * * *

A phone rings: "Hello."

"Hello, is this Mrs. Hickman?

"Yes."

"I'm Evelyn Smith, Ed's mother."

"Oh, yes, how are you?

"Not doing well, I'm afraid… But I thought you should know about the death of my son last night."

"OH NO! I'm so sorry."

After some uncomfortable silence, Mrs. Hickman asked, "Wasn't our Bobby at your house last night with Ed?"

"Yes, but after Ed took Bobby home, he went for a drive, and it was out there that he was in an accident with a big truck."

"I feel for you, Mrs. Smith. I don't know what to say."

"There's nothing to say, but you'll have to tell Bobby what happened, and that probably won't be easy."

"No, it won't. Thanks for calling."

"You're welcome, good-bye."

As Mrs. Hickman was hanging up, she thought of the daunting job she had before her.

* * * *

(The previous evening):

"Look, all you have to do is be at the wrong place at the wrong time," Bobby said as he snuffed out a smoldering Lucky Strike.

"The same goes for you. On your way home tonight you could get squashed by a semi-truck," replied Ed.

"That could happen to anyone."

Ed raised to a sitting position and looked at Bobby on the bed across from him and said, "I'm not saying that something *is* going to happen to you. All I'm saying is that you should be prepared in case it does."

In response Bobby said, "And how should I do that, Mr. Responsible?"

"Well, in the event that you get squashed by a semi on your way home tonight, why don't you write me out a will for your car?"

"Yeah, right."

That October night in 1964 they sat around arguing, talking about old times, drinking Brew 102, and listening to their favorite album, *The Paragons Meet the Jesters*. It was getting late, so Ed took Bobby home and went for the fateful drive.

* * * *

Irma Hickman pondered the dreadful task of telling her son what happened to Ed. Meanwhile, she told her husband and asked if he'd like to tell him, but he declined, believing that a woman's approach would be more soothing than anything he could come up with.

"Coward!" she said.

"I know, but there's some truth in my reasoning."

"Perhaps."

Bobby got up with a hangover, took a shower, and started getting ready for work at Denny's Coffee shop. When he greeted his mom, he could tell she was upset.

"What's wrong with you, Mom, you don't look so good?"

"Son, Ed's mother called this morning."

"Why?"

"Because she wanted me to tell you that Ed was killed last night in a terrible car accident."

"Oh shit! I thought he was going back home after he dropped me off. What happened?

"I guess he took a ride and collided with a big truck."

As the shock came across his face," Bobby said, "I'm calling work and taking off today.

"Good idea, son."

After he called in, he got in his old Studebaker and went to their friend Huck's house where they mourned Ed's demise with pot and beer.

About a month later, Bobby started having vivid dreams about Ed. They weren't the disjointed and confusing type of dreams that he and everyone else has. The dreams were as though he was watching Ed's life as though he was the one that died. This went on for a couple weeks. Every night he seemed to be watching Ed's life as he mourned Bobby. In his waking life, he was mourning Ed. It wasn't long before his waking mind was merging with his dreaming mind. Thoughts rather than dreams about Ed's life were intruding. *Damn!* He thought, *what the hell am I going through? I know, it's because of all the fucking drugs and alcohol.*

That was a logical conclusion but that wasn't it. He abstained from chemical substances for a couple weeks thinking the thoughts and dreams would subside but they didn't. They were, in fact, even more clear and vivid. He went back to the drugs and alcohol, but that only made things more confusing, so he stopped again, and again the thoughts and dreams became clear and vivid.

One night Bobby was at home watching television when a program came on focusing on theoretical physics. It wasn't anything he was usually interested in, but there were aspects of it that caught his attention for some reason. Trying to focus on the television program was difficult because Ed's life kept intruding.

Bobby lost his concentration completely when he clearly witnessed in his mind Ed looking out of his bedroom window and saw Huck pull up in his old Chevy. He then watched Ed leave the house, and get in Huck's car. He then watched the following scenario in his mind—like an alternate form of thinking.

Once in the car with Huck, Ed shivered and said, "Turn on

the fucking heater, what's wrong with you?"

"The fuckin heater doesn't work."

"Why don't you fix it then?"

"Why don't you fix it for me?"

"You're the mechanic. Besides, it's your car."

"You're the one that's cold."

"I don't know how to fix it."

"Stupid fucker, aren't ya?"

"Just go to the store okay, I'm thirsty." Ed said as he lit a Lucky.

"What store?"

"Farmer's Market, that's the only place they'll sell it to me."

"Why didn't you say so in the first place? Now I have to turn around and go back the other way."

"If your heater was working, I would have."

"Oh, another thing; I need gas," said Huck.

"Okay, I'll put some in. Want me to buy you a new heater, too?"

"Why that's mighty nice of you. Would you install it for me?"

"Yeah sure. Listen asshole, all I want to do is get drunk, so I can put up with you."

They pulled up to the market and Ed jumped out and entered the store.

Huck turned on his radio and started looking for a radio station. Suddenly the Beatles were singing I Want to Hold Your Hand," then just for the hell of it he reached over and switched on the heater. He thought to himself, "I'll be damned! It must be an electrical short." Then he smiled and thought, "he's gonna be pissed when he gets back in."

27

Ed opened the passenger door and sat the case of Brew 102 on the seat between them. Before he got in, he heard the heater's fan motor. He looked at the heater, then he looked at Huck with that, you son-of-a-bitch, look on his face.

"Well? Get in. What are you just standing there looking stupid for?" Then Huck started laughing.

When Ed got in and closed the door, Huck started the car and peeled out—tires screeching as they hit the pavement. He hit second gear and scratched again. Ed was still just sitting there staring at him blankly when Huck started slowing down, "what's wrong with you? Open me a beer, I'm thirsty. And don't start sniveling about it being cold in here, either. I felt sorry for you and fixed the heater."

Ed was still staring at him.

Then Huck added, "now you don't have to buy me a heater," and he started laughing again.

* * * *

Snapping out of his reverie, Bobby noticed that the television program wasn't making any sense now. He missed too much. He did recall the part that initially caught his attention. Something about the way subatomic particles behave. About a week later, he read a short article in a magazine entitled "Parallel Universes."

Wow! He thought, *that is some weird stuff. I wonder if that has anything to do with what I'm going through. I think I'll read up on it.*

One evening before going to bed, he thought he'd try something. Observing Ed in his bedroom, apparently drunk and playing their favorite song, "Let's Start All Over Again," Bobby wondered what would happen if he spoke to him rather than simply thinking about him. Since all this is going on in my mind, I'll simply speak directly to him silently.

28

"Ed, let's really do start all over again."

Bobby could tell by Ed's facial expression that he heard him, but not clearly, so he thought it best to not take it any further right then. He decided to try again later, after doing some research in the county library.

About a month later, after having spent some time at the library reading about theoretical physics, Bobby observed Ed drunk again in his bedroom playing their song.

What happened next took Ed by surprise. This time, as clear as if *Bobby* were in the room with him, Ed heard Bobby's voice in his mind.

"Ed? Like our song says, let's start all over again. We have to get reacquainted, ole buddy."

Without uttering a word, Ed replied, *Okay, Bobby, dead person, talk to me."*

"Wise Ass! You're drunk."

"I was drunk the last time you did this, too."

"I know Ed. I decided to approach you when you're drinking, so you wouldn't think you were losing your mind. This way, you could blame it on drugs and alcohol. I'm sure you can understand that."

"Why though?" Ed asked, slurring his words.

"Why what?"

"Why this? Why me? Why you? Why is all this happening?"

"It happens to everyone, Ed, but for some reason, you and I are consciously aware of it."

"I don't understand."

"I know, and neither did I until recently, but first get some sleep. You've got a good buzz on right now. We can continue this conversation when your head is clearer."

"Okay Bobby, dead person, I am sleepy, but I don't know

29

that I'll be able to sleep."

Ed went to sleep, but when he got up the next morning, he didn't know whether he had a very vivid dream, or he was really having a conversation with his dead friend.

The next morning when Ed heard his friend's voice in his mind, he replied with his mind: *"As a matter of fact, I do have a hangover, but that's beside the point. What I want to know is how I can be having a conversation with a dead person without opening my mouth?"*

"Like our favorite song says—let's start all over again. I could overdose you with all this right now, but I won't, so we're gonna have to take it easy. Okay?

"Yeah. I'm not in much of a position to argue with you."

"How are you feeling with all this?" Bobby Asked.

"How would you feel? I don't know . . ., but I guess I'm relieved in a way, because in a way, you're not really dead now."

"Well, the fact is, I'm not dead."

"Is that right? Then why did I see you in a coffin at your funeral?"

"Why don't you get adjusted to the fact that we're really communicating before I start explaining what's happening. Is that okay with you?"

"Yeah, I guess," Ed replied reluctantly.

"Do you think you can get comfortable with all of this?"

"I think so. I don't think I'm going to end up in the funny farm, if that's what you mean. I guess the shock is starting to wear off."

"Good. Then you understand why I've done this gradually and when you were drunk, and not too much at a time?"

"Yeah, I guess I do. You always were one to take advantage

30

of a drunk, asshole."

"*Good,*" said Bobby, a little relieved. "*I'm glad you called me asshole. I'm taking that to mean you're getting somewhat used to me again. I just can't explain everything to you right now Ed, so I'll talk to you later, okay?*"

"Finding all this difficult to digest, he reluctantly replied, "*Okay.*" Ed then lay down on his bed with his mind reeling, but after what seemed like an interminable amount of time, he finally did go to sleep.

* * * *

After about a month, Ed wondered why Bobby hadn't spoke to him lately? He also wondered why he couldn't initiate conversations with Bobby, rather than just the other way around. He added those questions to his list for the next time they talked.

When Bobby sensed that Ed might be getting a little squirrely, he decided to do what he'd been putting off since he found out what was happening to them, so he initiated contact: "*Hey old buddy, what'cha doin'?*

"*Bout fucking time you showed up. I was starting to question my sanity.*"

"*That's why I'm here now—to start explaining things to you,*" said Bobby as though he had all the answers. The truth was, he was being forced to explain what he was learning as he learned it, otherwise he'd be keeping Ed in the dark too long. Plus, he wasn't really sure how everything worked.

"*Okay, start explaining.*"

"*Well, this is going to be very similar to going back to school because, first of all, I have to enlighten you on some of the aspects of the theoretical side of quantum physics.*"

"*Oh Shit! Science? My worst subject in school besides math. How technical is it going to be?*"

31

"There's two sides to quantum physics, also known as quantum mechanics. There's the technical side which deals with a lot of charts, graphs, and mathematical theorems and equations. Don't sweat that side of it. Like I said, this is all about the theoretical side, which are unproven theories or possibilities."

"Whatever man, lay it on me. Regardless of how difficult it's going to be, I really do need to know."

"Alright then. Oh, some people, usually physicists, also refer to this as particle physics because it deals so much with atomic particles."

"So, what we're dealing with here are theories and possibilities, and this type of stuff is referred to as quantum physics, quantum mechanics, and particle physics. Is that right?

"Yes, that's right."

"Bobby, I'm gonna have to repeat a lot of this back to you to make sure I understand, so it's probably going to be slow-going. In other words, you're gonna have to spoon-feed this stuff to me."

"That's okay, whatever it takes. I agree, you need to understand." What Ed didn't know was that Bobby didn't know that much about all this himself, but he didn't want Ed to know that–at least not yet. *"First of all you should know what a particle is."*

"Hey," said Ed enthusiastically, *"I think I know. Isn't that those little cue ball things that bounce around inside of an atom?"*

"Yeah, electrons, neutrons, protons, photons, leptons, and the like. Since you know what they are, I'll tell you what they do. They are known for four basic abilities: A quantum particle can (1) be in two places at the same time, (2) doesn't exist until it is observed, (3) can travel from one place to another without going through the intervening space, (4) can influence other

particles at a distance."

"Hold on, Bobby. Let me get a pen and paper and write this shit down. Plus, I need to study it a bit."

"That's okay, take your time."

Ed went into his dad's room, which was also his office for the security patrol, and got a pen and some paper. When he returned, he asked Bobby to repeat those four things slowly so he could write them down. *"Okay Bobby, go on."*

"Well, those four things are important because when you think about each one on the micro level, it's . . ."

"Micro, that's very small right, like microscopic?"

"Yeah. So, when thinking about particles which are at the micro level, then a question arises: how much of that behavior is going on at the meso level–the level where we live in our daily lives, or even the macro level of the cosmos?

"Whoa, now you're talking science fiction, Bobby."

"Hey, it's a well known fact that theoretical physics is a whole lot more stranger and bizarre than science fiction. Science fiction is probably easier to swallow than this shit."

"Hmm. Yeah. Okay, go on."

"This is all, at least for now," said Bobby, *"before I start explaining the rest of it."*

"Alright, I'll think about what I've written down. Maybe I'll go to the library and see what else I can learn."

"Good, talk to you later."

A few minutes later Ed's dad opened the door, walked in and said, "I need your help on something"

"Okay dad, I'll be right there."

"To make more sense of all this, it's better that I speak out loud to you when I can," Ed explained. *"If I communicate with*

33

you about all this quantum stuff in my head, I'm afraid I won't absorb it as well."

"That makes sense."

"I gotta go, my dad wants me to do something for him. Hey, I meant to ask you something. Can I initiate contact with you rather than it being only you contacting me?"

"You'll have to practice by thinking hard about me and addressing me in your mind. At first, I won't hear you very clearly, but after awhile I will. You just need to practice."

"Okay, later."

Bobby went outside where W.R. was washing his car. He needed to talk with someone he could see. As W.R. was soaping down the hood of his car, Bobby grabbed the hose and said, "You wash, Dub, and I'll hose it off."

Meanwhile, Ed went to help his dad by typing monthly statements for his dad's security patrol. Ed knew how to type, but it was still a daunting job, because Mr. Smith had over 50 customers. When Ed was in high school, he took a typing course so he wouldn't have to do the one-finger poke, like his dad.

* * * *

A couple nights later while Ed was driving around in his car drinking beer, he pulled off the old highway between Barstow and Lenwood onto a dirt road and parked. Focusing on Bobby as intently as he could, he silently said, *"Hey Bobby, Dead Person."*

At the same time, Bobby was just pulling in to the Burger Haven, the local hangout, to get something to eat. As he parked, he thought he could hear something intruding on his thoughts. As he got out of the car, he again heard something that he thought sounded like someone saying, dead person. He immediately turned around, got back in his car thinking intently about Ed, and mentally said, *"Is that you?"*

34

"Yeah, who did you think it was?"

"I heard you," replied Bobby as he turned down the radio, *"but it was faint. Early on, if you hadn't referred to me as Dead Person, I probably wouldn't have realized that this was your first and weak attempt at contacting me, but that's okay, keep focusing real hard and you'll get it."* Then Bobby continued his side of the conversation by giving Ed some pointers that he found useful when he was first developing his ability to make contact. They then temporarily terminated their conversation.

About an hour later, Ed repeated, *"Hey dead person! Can you hear me now?"*

Bobby replied, *"Yes, I think you've got it down. I heard you plainly that time."*

"Good deal. It was a bummer that only you could contact me."

"I'm glad you've got it down. Hey, let me contact you tomorrow or the next day. I have something I have to do right now," said Bobby.

"Do!" Ed said questioningly. *Do what? Where are you? I don't get it. I remember you saying something about you not being dead, but all this quantum stuff doesn't explain that.*

"It will, old buddy, but those answers will have to wait. Later."

"Ass hole!"

"I heard that," quipped Bobby, *"Like I said, later."*

"Okay, later.

Bobby wanted to review what he'd been learning, getting it all straightened out, so he could be in a position to explain everything to Ed with the least confusion as possible. Theoretical physics isn't something he was ever interested in, but at this point in his life, he didn't have a choice.

CHAPTER THREE

Phenomenon

Bobby naturally wondered how he was able to equate a television program about theoretical physics to his own life when his knowledge about such things was about as close to nothing as possible. He was about to find out. One night as he was about to doze off, he heard a voice in his mind that wasn't Ed's.

"Hello Bobby."

No response. He needed to think for a minute. Thinking that there might be some answers coming from this very familiar female voice, he decided that it would be stupid not to say something. *"Hello to you, too. Your voice sounds familiar?"*

"Yes. I'm the only person you know, or have known, that has died.

"Grandma! Wow! What a surprise. I'd ask how you've been but you couldn't possibly still be alive in any universe."

"You're right dear, at least from your perspective, but I don't want to get into that right now. Anyway, I see that you were able to attribute the information in that television program to what's happening in your life."

"I was grasping at straws, Grandma. I was just using that information to try to make sense of all this, but I'm still not very clear on all of it."

"I know," said Bobby's grandma, *"so let's focus on the information in that television program and how that's connected to what's happening in your life."*

"Okay."

"You're on the right track, but I must admit I kinda steered you in the right direction."

"And I thought my brilliant mind came up with it."

"Not quite, Bobby. I think you'll agree that what's important is to learn about what's happening to you and be in a position to explain it to Ed."

"Okay, I'm ready."

Armed with enough of the information he needed, it was now time to explain a few things to Ed. *"Okay, are you ready for a limited explanation?"*

As Ed was getting ready to park his car in front of his parents' house, he replied, *"I was ready for that the first night we spoke."*

"I know, sorry bout that, but at that time I wasn't capable of explaining it right, and I'm still not really, so you will have to do some reading at the library. I'm just going to tell you enough to explain why this is happening to us."

"Okay, dead person, enlighten me."

"Quit calling me dead person. I'm not dead."

"Really?" replied Ed, *"Then what are you?"*

"We'll get to that, but first, let me give you the short version."

After taking a swig of beer and lighting a cigarette, Ed replied, *"Alright, go ahead."*

"There's an experiment called the double slit experiment. Rather than go through all the technical shit, it's really only important that you be aware of the experiment. Okay, it was once an accepted fact that subatomic particles were made of matter, kinda like tiny little cue balls. However, as a result of the double slit experiment, it was revealed that particles are also waves. So then physicists wondered what particles were— particles of matter or particles of waves?

38

The answer is both, which is referred to as particle duality, but that isn't really the answer either. The fact is, physicists don't really know. It's a mystery. No one knows why particles behave this way. At first physicists believed that the wave wasn't real, that the wave somehow existed only in their minds as a way to explain experiments. They finally came to the conclusion that they were "waves of possibility" which they called the quantum wave function.

I realize, Ed, that this doesn't make much sense, so when I'm done here, you really should go to the library and look up the double slit experiment in a book about quantum physics. Once you do that, then my shorter version here will hopefully make more sense."

"You're right, it doesn't make much sense, but go on. I'll read up on it later if I need to know more."

"Good. Anyway, in the double slit experiment, only two worlds were necessary. In one world, the particle was projected through one slit. In the other world, the particle was projected through the other slit. The two worlds would exist side-by-side, completely separate from each other until the particles reached the screen of the experiment. Then the two worlds would overlap or merge. Why would the worlds merge on the screen after splitting apart? The answer was even stranger. Now this is where you and I come in, Ed. In this scenario, the wave represents not possibilities or likelihoods but realities. The wave is composed of particles in parallel worlds. Well, what's true in the micro world is thought to be true in the meso and macro worlds. As you know, micro means microscopic and not visible to the eye; the meso level is where we live in our daily lives and visible to the eye, and the macro level is the big picture of the cosmos. So Ed, I thought it best that I tell you what I just told you, rather than coming out of the blue with a statement like, "you and I are living in parallel universes."

"Wow! Are you telling me that we're both alive but in different worlds or universes?"

"Yes, that's the crux of it. Now, it's up to you, if you feel the need, to bone up on quantum physics and parallel universes. Either that, or simply accept what I'm saying and leave it at that."

"Hmm. This is a bit overwhelming. I think I'll do both. The fact is, we're having silent conversations, and I don't think I'm hallucinating, so I'm accepting what you're saying but I'll probably, eventually, bone up on all this.

"Good. I imagine you have more questions, huh?"

"Of course. So, in your world I'm the one that died, right?"

"Yeah. Like you, I attended a funeral and went through all the grief and other shit that you did.

They both explained to each other *what* they'd been going through in their respective worlds and agreed that they'd continue doing what they'd been doing. The only exception was the drinking and drug use. They agreed that it would be in their best interest to keep their heads as clear as possible.

"Now that you've explained the basics to Ed," said Bobby's grandma, *"I'm going to give you a thorough explanation of all the technical stuff."*

"Okay."

"When I'm done, I suggest you go to the library and read about it to make sure that I explained it right or I didn't leave anything out."

"Okay, grandma, I'm listening."

The phenomenon that grandma explained to Bobby is available in books on theoretical physics, but having it explained by someone makes it easier to understand.

Information from a book could easily leave one feeling a little detached from it, but here's the gist of what Bobby read, which made him better understand what grandma had told him.

The double slit experiment:

In the basic version of this experiment, a beam of light illuminates a plate with two parallel slits, and the light passing through the slits is observed on a screen behind the plate. The wave nature of light causes the light waves passing through the two slits to interfere with each other, producing bright and dark bands on the screen—a result that would not be expected if light consisted of classical particles of matter. The same effect can be observed on the bottom of a pool when two drops or pebbles disturb the sunny and otherwise smooth surface of the water. In the experiment, the waves spreading from each disturbance meet and interfere with each other: where the crest of one wave meets the crest of the other, they reinforce each other and appear bright. Where the troughs meet they cancel each other out and appear dark.

Are the quantum particles that pass through the slits waves? If so, they could then pass through both slits and form interference patterns. This assumption makes sense until a weak light source is used in the experiments where only one photon is emitted at a time. Commonsense tells us that s single photon cannot be a wave—it must be a packet of energy of some sort. But then it should be able to pass through only one of the slits and not both slits at the same time. Yet when single photons are emitted, a wave interference pattern builds up on the screen, as if each photon had passed through both slits.

If light consisted strictly of ordinary or classical particles, and these particles were fired in a straight line through a slit and allowed to strike a screen on the other side, we would expect to see a pattern corresponding to the size and shape of the slit. However, when this "single-slit experiment" is actually performed, the pattern on the screen is a diffraction pattern in which the light is spread out. The smaller the slit, the greater the angle of spread, which is also inexplicable using the classical mechanics of, say, Einstein's theories. The discovery of quantum physics defies what was previously thought of as the

41

last word on what is now referred to as classical physics.

So, are subatomic particles made of matter or waves? The answer is both, which is referred to as particle duality, but that isn't really the answer either. The fact is, physicists don't really know. It's a mystery. No one knows why particles behave this way. At first physicists believed that the wave wasn't real, that the wave somehow existed only in their minds as a way to explain experiments. They finally came to the conclusion that they were "waves of possibility" which they called the quantum wave function or probability wave. So, in the double slit experiment, there was really only one particle present at any time near the slits, and the wave represented the different possibilities that the particle had. In this way, one explained that only the possibility or, in the language of quantum physics, the probability, of that particle moving through the slits was determined. One could not predict where a particle was likely to go. When there were two slits open, the particle had two ways to go.

Parallel Universes:

In 1957 a graduate student came up with the weird idea that physicists should take quantum physics seriously. If it says that two alternatives can interfere with each other, then somehow those alternatives must both exist at the same time. If possibilities can affect each other, if two or more probabilities can in some way add up, then in some way these possibilities should really exist somewhere. But where?

In the double slit experiment, only two worlds were necessary. In one world, the particle passed through one slit. In the other world, the particle passed through the other slit. The two worlds would exist side-by-side, completely separate from each other until the particle reached the screen. Then the two worlds would overlap or merge. Why would the worlds merge after splitting apart? The answer was even more weird, although

42

it did satisfy the question.

The answer to the question was self-consistency. This was the only way in which the interference could be explained and still have only one particle. The universe itself was continually doing this splitting and merging every time that anything interacted with anything else. Each split was necessary to produce the wave behavior and each merger was necessary to produce the particle.

According to this explanation, the wave represents not possibilities or likelihoods but realities—an infinite number of them. The wave is composed of particles in parallel worlds. When the particle strikes the slits, the world, the whole universe containing it splits into two or a multiplicity of mutually unobservable but equally real worlds.

* * * *

"Hey Ed."

"Yeah, I was just thinking about contacting you."

"Oh yeah, about what?"

"About the outrageous metaverse of parallel worlds."

"That's good. Tell me about it—the short version."

"Okay. The metaverse, which is 'parallel universes' abbreviated, is described as an infinite series of existences, in a dizzily growing, ever spreading network of diverging, converging and parallel universes or existences. This web of time—the strands of which approach one another, divide, intersect or ignore each other through the centuries—embraces every possibility. We do not exist in most of them. In some you exist and I don't, while in others I exist and you don't, and in others both of us exist. How's that?

"Sounds to me like something you got out of a book."

"It is. That didn't come from me. I read it to you out of the

book that's sitting right here in front of me, but it explains it pretty well for a short version."

"Yeah, it does, but now I have a confession to make, Ed."

"You're not going to tell me this is all a big joke, are you?

"No, but I am going to admit that you now know about as much about all this as I do."

"Hmm, the blind leading the blind, huh?"

"Yeah, I guess you can think of it that way. You see, there's been someone explaining to me everything that I've been explaining to you."

"Who's that?" asked Ed.

"My grandma who died a long time ago."

"Okay, but she's not alive in another universe, right?" asked Ed.

"I don't think so. I don't think people can live that long. Anyway, you've probably noticed that communication between us, and all anthropomorphics for that matter, are limited to people who are dead in all the existences involved. For example, if my grandma is dead in my existence or universe and alive in yours, this phenomenon wouldn't work."

"That didn't occur to me, but it makes sense. And what was that big word you used to describe us?

"Oh shit–I guess I forgot that little piece of information. Anyway, I don't know who selected the word, anthropomorphic, but that's the word my grandma used to describe us. I looked it up in the dictionary. Here's how the dictionary defines it: "Attribution of human motivation, characteristics, or behavior to inanimate objects, animals, or natural phenomena." Evidently, we are the natural phenomena."

"I've never thought of myself as a phenomenon, and I wouldn't think of all this as natural either," said Ed.

"Me either."

"So, we are anthropomorphics, and we all live in separate worlds or existences or universes, right?"

"Right."

"And the three words—worlds, existences, and universes are used interchangeably, right?

"I think so. It's possible that we'll find one of those words more descriptive in various contexts. I guess we'll find out as we learn and experience more."

CHAPTER FOUR

Work and Play

Time passed–about two years of it. It was 1966 and Bobby and Ed were still learning things about the workings of anthropomorphics. They decided that using that long word in dialogue was cumbersome, so they agreed to abbreviate anthropomorphic to anthro or anthros, depending on context.

In Baker, California the gusty March winds provided Ed with an unexpected day off. He had been working as a laborer on a local construction site. Ed's father had acquired him the job, drove him to Baker, and got him settled in. Because Ed's license had been revoked as a result of a DUI conviction, he left his car parked at his parents' house. The construction job was only going to last to the end of the summer. Around that time his driving privilege would be restored.

Baker is located 60 miles north of Barstow and 90 miles south of Las Vegas, Nevada. The little town serves as a tourist trap for travelers en-route to Vegas. The population is approximately two hundred people-all of which work in various service stations, restaurants, garages and construction sites such as the one Ed was employed with.

Baker's locale was in such a desolate area that the construction company furnished rooms for the crew. These sleeping quarters were contained in a very old two story ramshackle rooming house.

One day Ed was kicked back in his room, bored with his unexpected day off. His friend Jimbo came to mind, and he wondered if he could get him a job there, too. Ed went downstairs to room one where the foreman resided to ask.

The forty year old foreman was a big burly redneck with a full beard and a paunch who went by the name of Butch.

Ed knocked on the door, and when Butch answered, he said, "Hi Kid, how ya hangin?"

"Oh, pretty good, sir. Was wondering if I could talk to you?"

Butch motioned for Ed to come in as he replied, "You've only been on the job three days, kid, you can't have a raise yet or an advance." Then Butch laughed, and took a drink of his beer.

"It's not that," Ed said in response as he followed Butch into the untidy rubble of his room.

"Have a seat, kid."

Ed started to sit down on the bed when Butch said, "Watch out for crabs though."

Ed immediately jumped up with a funny look on his face. When Butch saw that, he burst into laughter. He gestured with his arm for Ed to sit down as he said, "Just kidding, kid, don't take me serious unless we're on the job. Now what can I do for you?"

Ed looked at Butch with a mixture of fear and awe, as he cautiously reclaimed his seat on the bed and ask, "I have a friend who needs a job. Do you have room for another man?"

Butch opened a small ice box and grabbed another beer. As he took a church key and opened it, he looked at Ed seriously and said, "Now that's what I call timing, kid. Yes I do, because I'm firing you Friday."

When Ed's eyes grew as large as watermelons, Butch couldn't keep from laughing again and said, "I told you not to take me serious unless we're on the job." Butch shook his head, still laughing and said, "Have him on the job site Monday morning, kid."

Ed stood up and started for the door, being glad it was time to get away from this lunatic. "Thanks, sir, see you in the morning," Ed said as he was getting ready to open the door and get the hell out of there.

"Hey kid, tell your friend he can room with you. There isn't anybody in there with you, is there?"

"No, just the crabs" replied Ed with a smile.

All the rooms had two single beds in them. Sleeping rooms were all they really were with toilet facilities down the hall.

"Okay, kid, see you in the morning if you don't get bit by a scorpion or sidewinder."

Ed laughed and shook his head as he closed the door thinking, *"What a fucking character!"* He then went to a pay phone to call Jimbo.

Ed told him to be in Baker on Sunday.

When Sunday rolled around, Ed was in his room reading a Las Vegas magazine when there was a knock on the door. He knew who it was as he opened the door and said, "I'm sure glad to see you, Ole Buddy; that is if you brought some beer money."

"Yeah, I have some money." Replied Jimbo as he looked at the cramped quarters.

"Well, gimmy some, and I'll go to the store while you get settled in."

"Jimbo got out his wallet, gave Ed some money, and said, "Get a couple packs of smokes, too."

"Okay, be right back."

About an hour later when they were about half way through their case of beer, Jimbo said, "I have a surprise out in my car. I'll be right back."

When he returned, he reached into his shirt pocket and pulled out a joint, held it up in the air and said, "See."

"You mean you had this out there this whole time?" Ed asked, as though he couldn't believe it.

"No, the marijuana fairy stashed it in my car a few minutes ago?" replied Jimbo.

"Well, thank the marijuana fairy for me and light it up!"

After Ed took the last toke and ate the roach, he looked at Jimbo and said, "This is good shit."

"Yeah, those marijuana fairies get the best."

At six o'clock the next morning Ed and Jimbo were on the job with hangovers. It was hard work, and they were tired when they got off work.

The union pay scale in 1966 was approximately $3.75 an hour. Since they weren't in the union, they were being paid $3.00 an hour. For them at the time, that was good money. Neither of them was accustomed to anything other than minimum wage jobs, which was $1.40 an hour at the time.

They worked all week and Friday finally arrived. Payday for Ed, but Jimbo had to wait another week, because the first week's paycheck was withheld, just as the previous week's check was withheld from Ed.

It was quitting time and Butch, the foreman, had delivered Ed's check to him just prior to quitting time. When Jimbo and Ed met at Jimbo's car, Jimbo asked, "Did you get your check?"

"Yep," replied Ed with a big smile, "Take me to the Baker Market and I'll cash it."

Jimbo started his car and said, "You got it." Then he popped the clutch, and started fish tailing from the job site."

Ed went into the Baker market, cashed his check, and bought a case of beer and cigarettes. When he returned to the car, he got in and counted it, then handed half of it to his friend and said, "Here, this is half of my pay check, so I expect half of yours next Friday, okay?"

"Wait just a fucking minute. Don't piss on my back, and tell me I'm sweating. You didn't get a full pay check, fucker!"

50

"Oh," replied Ed sheepishly. "I forgot."

"Nice try, though."

"I didn't try that on purpose."

"Yeah right," replied Jimbo.

They took their beer and smokes to their room and took turns using the shower down the hall. When Ed returned from his shower, he asked, "Hey man, let's go to Ash Meadows. What do you say?"

"You took the words right out of my mouth," Jimbo replied as he grabbed his towel and soap.

Ash Meadows was a ranch with a small landing strip, cocktail lounge, motel, and a whore house. It was located seven miles northeast of Death Valley Junction which is approximately 90 miles northwest of Baker. Prostitution was and still is legal in various counties of Nevada.

When Jimbo returned from his shower, Ed asked, "Do you still have that ice chest in the trunk of your car?"

"I do."

"Well, let's gas up and get a quick hamburger and some ice for the beer and get the hell out of this little hell-hole of a town."

Off they went out of Baker on highway 127, tires smoking, radio blaring, and sucking down beers. With high spirits and money in their pockets, they argued and carried on as usual.

About 60 miles out of Baker, they had a flat tire. While sitting on the side of the road, neither of them was feeling any pain. Ed took a coin out of his pocket and said, "Call it."

"Heads."

"Shit!" said Ed, noticing that Jimbo was on the verge of laughter.

Jimbo was still smiling evil-like as Ed snatched the keys out of the ignition and got out to go change the tire.

51

Before Ed closed the car door, he asked, "What's that shit eating grin on your face for, anyway?" Without waiting for an answer, he went back to open the trunk.

Still smiling, Jimbo listened for the trunk to open, and then he waited for it.

"You fuckin ass-hole!" Ed screamed. "You knew when I flipped that coin the fucking spare was flat."

When Ed came back around to the passenger side and looked in, Jimbo was snickering.

"You're about the dumbest, most worthless excuse of an ass-hole I've ever known in my life! Why would you carry around a spare tire with no fucking air in it? I'll tell you why, because you're a fucking moron, an imbecile, a fucking retarded half-wit idiot! Now you can take that fucking flat tire and hitchhike back to Baker, or walk for that matter, and get it fixed."

With the grin still on his face, Jimbo asked, "You wanna flip for it?"

"Fuck you! I'm not going anywhere, so hit the fucking road dip shit."

"Okay, okay, damn you drive a hard bargain."

* * * *

"*Bobby?*" Ed asked silently when Jimbo was down the road a ways, "*Now what?*"

"*Now what, what?*" Bobby replied.

"*What if Jimbo can't get the tire fixed?*"

"*I guess you'll just be stuck, I guess.*"

"*A lot of help you are,*" Ed said as he got out of the car."

"*I suppose I could make a suggestion.*"

"*That would be nice.*"

52

"Okay, uh, go for a walk," said Bobby, *"it's a beautiful night."*

Irritated and slurring his words from drinking, Ed asked, "That's your fucking suggestion?"

"Hold on, stupid, I'm not finished. On your walk look for animals. Any kind of animals. Even large insects or birds. When or if you find any, try to think of a way they could possibly help you."

Ed waited momentarily and asked, *"Are you serious?"*

"I really am."

"Okay, then what?" Ed asked as he lit a cigarette and started walking around the car.

"When you find a creature of some kind, start thinking in terms of how that creature could help you."

"Then what?" asked Ed getting more frustrated.

"That's it."

"What do you mean, that's it?"

"Just what I said. That's it."

"Bobby, you're crazier dead than you were alive . . . Hey . . . ! Hey Bobby . . . Shit! You ass-hole!" Then Ed mumbled to himself, "Go find animals, bugs or birds. Ha!"

Dumbfounded and still half drunk, Ed started staggering down the desolate two lane highway in the opposite direction that Jimbo had gone. Ed walked for about fifteen minutes and came upon a dirt road that went west, so he started following it. About five minutes later he came to a barbed wire fence that went south towards Baker. He continued for awhile longer enjoying the bright full moon-lit night with the stars twinkling brightly above, when he came upon a herd of cattle grazing on the other side of the fence. As he continued walking, he felt himself starting to sober up a little, and thought how neat it would be if one of those cows would follow him back to the car and lay down in the middle of the road so an oncoming car would have to at least slow down enough for him to get the driver's attention. About that time something strange happened. He stopped walking long enough to light a cigarette. Then, when he threw the match down, he was looking into the eyes of a cow. The cow even seemed ironically aware of it. They held eye contact for about ten seconds, then he realized what he was doing. Finding the experience rather ludicrous, he just figured he wasn't starting to sober up after all, so he shrugged it off and turned around and started walking back.

As he was walking, he turned his head, and out of the corner of his eye, he thought he saw something. Realizing what he thought he saw, he jerked his head back again and stopped dead in his tracks. The cow seemed to be following him. He got closer to the cow, and again he and the cow held eye contact for a few seconds. Ed walked a little farther, keeping the cow in check, then came to realize that the cow was, indeed, following him. Not knowing what to think about such a thing, he came upon the place where he first encountered the barbed wire fence. Ed stopped and pondered the situation. That cow had left the rest of the herd to follow him, even though he was on the other side of the fence. Now he had come to the end of it, preventing the cow from being able to follow him any farther. Ed scratched his head and thought about his previous fantasy about the cow following him to the car and laying down in the road. He also thought about what Bobby said concerning animals. With nothing to lose, he hoped that the cow would stay put until he returned with a pair of wire cutters or something to cut the fence with.

Ed finally returned to the fence with a pair of wire cutters from Jimbo's tool box. As he approached the fence, he found the cow was still standing there as if he were actually waiting for his return. Ed walked over and snipped the three strands of barbed wire, and then looked at the cow, again making eye contact. Ed smiled at the cow, turned around and continued walking back towards the car, wondering if the cow would follow. Ed walked about twenty feet, looked around to see, and sure enough, he was.

Back at the car, Ed opened the trunk and replaced the wire cutters. When he closed it, he turned around and looked for the cow. At first he couldn't see him, but soon noticed that the cow had, indeed, laid down right there in the middle of the highway, about ten yards behind the car. He couldn't believe it. In fact, the whole affair was amazing. Suddenly, he started laughing. When his laughter subsided, he thought to himself: *and I can't even tell anybody, not even Jimbo. He'd definitely think I snapped.* That's what made it so easy to keep the secret. Who'd believe it?

After sitting in the car for awhile, Ed saw car lights in the rear view mirror, so he got out and walked a little ways towards it. The cow was still laying there. The oncoming car had to come to a slow speed when the driver's high beams brought the cow into view. As the car came closer, Ed approached the driver and said, "I don't know why that stupid cow decided to take a nap right there."

"You mean that cow is alive?" said the middle aged man with a receding hair line and a conservative mustache.

"Yeah," Ed said as he walked up to the man, "She's just laying there sound asleep."

"Really?"

"Yeah, c'mon look for yourself."

"People sometimes hit livestock in this area. It's pretty common, actually," the man said, still not convinced that the cow was asleep.

"I'm aware of that, but that cow ain't dead. C'mon," Ed replied as motioned for the man to follow.

"That's O.K., I believe you. I....."

Then before the guy had a chance to say anything more, Ed asked, "Say, I wonder if you would consider helping me out, sir?"

"If I can. What's the problem?" The man replied as he looked at the cow again.

"Flat tire, and my half-wit friend's spare is flat, so he took off walking with the tire to see if he could get it fixed."

As Ed was talking with the man, he noticed that the man wore glasses and was wearing a suit.

"Yes," The man replied, "I passed him. He even tried to flag me down, but I don't stop for anybody out here in no man's land. Lucky for you that cow is there."

"Yeah, I'll say."

"Are you sure that cow is alive?" The man asked again.

"Go see for yourself."

The man just shook his head and said, "Strange damn thing for a cow to do." Then the man diverted his attention to Ed's problem and said, "Jump in son, and let's get up there closer to your car." The man drove around the sleeping cow and pulled up next to Jimbo's car and asked, "That's a 57 Chevy isn't it?"

"Yes, sir."

"Well, this car I'm driving is a 63 Chevy and the wheels are interchangeable, so I'll just give you the spare. This is a rented car so they'll never know the difference."

"What if you have a flat?"

"I'll just call the auto club."

"Out here!" Ed asked.

"Yeah, that could be a problem," The man said as he laughed. "I'll take my chances. Besides, they usually keep good tires on these rentals."

"I sure do appreciate this, sir."

Just then they both turned their heads simultaneously to look at the cow, but the cow was gone. Then they just looked at each other, amazed. The man then got out of his car, got the spare out, then got back into his car, started it and said, "Good luck, son."

"Yeah," Ed replied, "Good luck to you too, and thanks again."

The man said, "You're welcome," and he drove away.

* * * *

It was about eight O'clock by the time Ed got the tire changed, and he drove to where Jimbo was still walking.

When Ed pulled up and stopped, Jimbo opened the passenger door and placed the tire between the front and back seat. When Jimbo got in, he asked, "How did you get that car to stop?"

"What makes you think that car stopped?"

"Because I don't believe in fairy godmothers."

"Do you still want to go to the whore house?" Ed asked as he put the car in low gear and flipped a U.

"Hell yeah," Jimbo replied, "And I want to know how you got that car to stop?"

"My fairy godmother did it for me."

"Why do you want to fuck with me after I walked all that way?"

"Why not?"

"Fuck it then, I ain't going to share this joint with you then."

"What joint?" Ed asked excitedly.

"The one that my fairy godmother brought me."

About a half an hour later they were driving down the dirt road that starts where California borders with Nevada. Ed

57

stopped the car and said, "I have to piss." When Ed was finished, he went around to the passenger side, opened the door, and said, "You drive."

Their high spirits had been restored, and they were arguing, cutting up, and laughing again when they pulled under the trees that serve as an entrance way to the ranch. There was a big swimming pool in front of the bar. To the right there was a large mobile home with a small wooden staircase leading to a door with a red light over it. They were stopped under the big trees when Jimbo said, "This is a nice place."

"Yeah, it is, but let's go in and have a beer in the bar first."

"Okay." Jimbo pulled over to the left and parked by the swimming pool.

The small bar was only big enough for the bar itself and some stools. As they took a seat at the bar, the bartender approached and said, "What'll it be guys?"

"I'll have a Coors," answered Jimbo.

"Me too," added Ed.

The bartender brought their drinks, and the guys paid the man individually. The bartender thanked them and walked back down to the other end of the bar, and continued his conversation with another patron.

Knowing that Jimbo was somewhat of a racist, Ed asked, "Are you going to pick a black woman?"

Jimbo just looked at him and said, "Yeah, right."

"I'll tell you what, I'll pay for it if you do."

"Fuck you," said Jimbo. "You probably would too, just so you could go tell everybody in Barstow."

"So what?"

"Well, I just as well they don't know I came here." Jimbo replied, his tone becoming more serious.

"I'm going to tell anyway, and I'm going to say that you chose a big ugly black woman."

"If you do, I'll fuck you up!" Jimbo said as Ed laughed.

They finished their beers and left.

They walked over to the door with the red light over it, and Ed said, "Here we are. Ready to go in and get your cherry popped?"

Before Jimbo had a chance to respond, the door opened and a big ugly jolly black madame was standing there, and instantly Ed started laughing again.

If looks could kill, Ed would've dropped dead on the spot. The madame spoke as she looked at Ed laughing, "Happy gentlemen, that's what we's like to see round heah. C'mon in, boy's. Yes suh, we's like happy menfolks. Makes our girls happy, too. You boys sits down an make yerselves comfy, and I's a git the girls fo ya."

The madame waddled off down a corridor, and Ed asked, "Jimbo, I's a payin if you'll take that big fine mammy right there."

Jimbo said in a hushed voice, "Shut the fuck up, here they come."

The madame came waddling back out of the corridor with five beauties following behind her. All of them sparsely dressed in bikini's and other suggestive clothing. They lined up in front of the boys who were seated on a sofa that sat next to a juke-box that was playing *Heart of Stone* by the Rolling Stones. Then the madam began her introduction with an ear-to-ear smile on her jolly face. She gestured towards the first one in the line-up which was a very pretty blonde with hair down to the bottom of her back. "This heah be Linda." Before the madam had a chance to continue the introduction, Ed interrupted and said, "I'll take Linda!"

The madam laughed and nodded towards the pretty blonde.

59

Then Linda said, "Follow me, Honey."

"Okay," Ed replied.

As Ed followed Linda into the corridor the madam continued her introduction. "And this heah be Wanda." The attractive brunette smiled pretty, and Jimbo nodded his head. The process continued until the introductions were complete.

Three hours later Jimbo and Ed were in their ramshackle rooming house sound asleep.

CHAPTER FIVE

Tijuana

Jimbo and Ed worked all summer until the job was finished. The foreman offered to keep them on, but the next job was located in northern California. They declined the offer because it was too far away and too cold up there.

Ed stayed in bed thinking before he got up to begin his day. He thought about how drastically his life had changed. Bobby's death was one thing, but this anthropomorphic phenomenon had been a challenge to digest. Having the ability to communicate between parallel universes and manipulate animal behavior weren't things that just anybody could do; that is, except for other anthros. Furthermore, he'd learned that there were, indeed more anthros. It wasn't as rare as he'd assumed.

With the money that Ed was able to save from working all summer, he started fixing up his car. Having had it lowered and painted, all he needed was upholstery, so he decided that Tijuana would be the place to get himself one of the fashionable tuck-n-roll jobs. The only thing he had to do was go to the DMV and get his license back because of the DUI.

Right after Ed took the driving test and got his temporary license, he called his friend.

"Is Huck there?"

"Just a minute, I'll see."

Moments later Huck came to the phone and said, "Hello."

"What are you doing?"

"Nothing. What are you doing?"

"I'm considering a trip to Tijuana. Wanna go?"

"Yeah, I guess. I don't have anything better to do."

"Okay, be there a little later."

When Ed pulled up and honked, Huck came out and got in the car. They bought a six pack of beer and got onto the freeway. As with most addicts, abstinence from chemical substances is short-lived. One would think, however, after just getting his license back, that he'd at least try to make an effort to abstain, but that's not the nature of the beast. They did make the six pack last the 190 miles to the border.

After dropping the car off at the upholstery shop, they walked to the nearest bar where they ordered a beer. After taking a swig out of his bottle of Corona, Ed asked, "Are you going to buy a piece of ass while you're here?"

"No, are you?"

"I'd like to but I'm too afraid of catching something."

"Well," said Huck after lighting a cigarette, "Look at that little cutie over there checking us out."

"Let's just finish this beer and get out of here before one of us weakens."

As they started for the door, the little cutie cut them off and asked, "Sucky fucky, big boys?"

In unison, they said "No!" as they walked out of the door.

"Rather than go through this in other bars, why don't we just get something to drink and go back to the upholstery shop and drink it," suggested Ed.

"Good idea."

After drinking a half pint of Bacardi 151 rum, they couldn't sit still, so they went for a walk through the downtown area where the majority of street-corner whores, nightclubs, and crazy taxi drivers were located.

"Hey Ed, isn't that Mike Blaisdell across the street talking to that old Mexican?"

"Wow! I think so," but by the time they got over there, Mike had walked into the bar that he and the Mexican were standing in front of.

"I guess we're gonna have to go into another bar," Ed said as he flipped a cigarette butt into the street.

By the time they got across the street, Mike had gone inside the bar. When they walked up to the barstool where Mike was sitting, Ed said, "What the fuck are you doing here, Mike?"

Turning around at the sound of his name, he looked at his old friends and said, "Huuh . . . I'll be damned. No tellin who's liable to show up down here."

"Yeah," replied Huck, "No tellin."

Mike got up and shook hands with his old friends, then asked, "So what brings you to my quaint little village?"

"Your quaint little village is where I'm getting tuck and roll for my car," replied Ed.

"Huuh . . . well, let's grab that table over there and celebrate," suggested Mike. As they were sitting down Mike looked toward the door and said, "Hey guys, I'm known down here as Sagus, not Mike. Can you guys remember that?"

Ed nodded and Huck replied, "Yeah, no problem."

Again glancing toward the door and back to his friends, Sagus added, "And don't mention my last name at all. I have a different one down here."

"Okay," Ed answered, "but why all the subterfuge?"

"Because I have warrants in the States, plus I'm involved in some tricky activity down here."

"Your secret is safe with me," said Huck.

63

"Me too." added Ed.

"Good," replied Sagus glancing at the door again. "Huuh . . . Now, if you don't mind, I need you guys to smuggle a couple pounds of heroin back into the States for me."

"WHAT!?"

"Just kidding," said Sagus, "don't get your bowels in an uproar. I wouldn't ask you to do anything like that."

"Is that the illegal activity you're into down here," asked Ed.

"No, but let's not talk about that. Tell me what's happenin in Barstow?" Sagus asked as he glanced at the door and motioned for the bartender to bring drinks.

"Nothing ever happens in Barstow," replied Huck as he looked around the sleazy bar room, "we're more interested in what's happenin here."

"Yeah," added Ed, "what's keeping you in Tijuana and why do you keep looking at the door?"

"Money keeps me here," replied Sagus, "and lots of drugs, sex, and rock n roll."

"That's pretty good incentive," said Huck, "but there's plenty of sex, drugs, and rock n roll in the States without all the disadvantages of a border town. It's my guess that you're running from a prison sentence in the States."

"You're right," admitted Sagus glancing at the door again, "Tijuana is a lot more fun than San Quentin."

"You did it again," said Huck.

"Did what?" asked Sagus.

"You keep looking at the door."

"Oh, that—huuh . . . well, I'm expecting someone."

"Would it be that old Mexican you were talking to before you came in here?" asked Ed.

"Yeah," replied Sagus as he stood up, "and there he is. I'll be right back guys, wait here."

As they waited for Sagus to return, Ed heard a familiar voice in his head: *"Hey Ed, what's happenin?"*

"Not now Bobby. I'll get back to ya, okay?"

"Okay."

Just as Ed and Huck were finishing their drinks, Sagus joined them again and motioned to the bartender for more drinks. When the bartender walked away, Huck asked, "You must have a tab here."

Yeah, I do," replied Sagus as he got up again. "Come with me, guys, we need more privacy."

Ed and Huck followed, and when they were inside a room, Sagus closed and locked the door and asked, "How do you like my office?"

As the guys looked around, Huck asked, "Your office or the bar's office?"

"I work out of this office so, yeah, it's my office," replied Sagus as he took a seat behind a desk. "Have a seat on that sofa over there and I'll tell you what's goin on."

"Good idea," said Ed as he and Huck sat down, "I hope there aren't any crabs hanging around on this old couch."

"Huuh . . . just think of them as potential pets."

Ed and Huck looked at each other, smiled, and then Huck shook his head and asked, "Okay you old crab farmer, what's all this cloak and dagger shit that's going on here with you?"

"Well, if I can't trust my homeboys with all this, who can I trust?"

"Trust us with *what* homeboy?" Ed asked as he lit a cigarette and got comfortable.

"Huuh . . . well . . . I need your help, so before you ask what

65

for, I'll start by saying that it could be dangerous–maybe even life-threatening," warned Sagus, then he asked, "Are you guys willing to take a chance on possibly being killed in Tijuana with nobody back home ever knowing what happened to you?"

Huck and Ed looked at each other, then Huck asked Ed what he thought about it.

"I'm game," replied Ed, "but I'd feel more comfortable calling someone back home, right now, telling them that we're down here getting my car upholstered."

Huck looked at Sagus and said, "Yeah, and if that's okay with you, then we'll at least hear you out."

"Okay with me guys, so go make your calls and I'll wait here," replied Sagus. "I'd let you use the phone here, but I'd rather not. No tellin who might be listening. There's a pay phone at the gas station down the street. You'll see it to the right when you walk out of the bar."

When they returned from making their phone calls, Ed said, "Okay, we're all ears."

"Well, huuh, uh . . . someone is going to kill me if I make another batch of counterfeit twenty dollar bills."

"Are you going to make another batch?" Ed asked.

"Yeah," replied Sagus as he opened a desk drawer and took a piece of paper out, "But I can't do it until I get my competition out of the way."

"What!" exclaimed Huck, "You want us to kill your competition?"

Sagus shook his head, laughed and said, "No, no, no . . . we need to come up with a way to get him busted or something to get him out of business."

Mocking Sagus, Ed replied by saying, "Huuh."

"Yeah, huuh," repeated Huck, and then added, "..and you want us to set him up, right?"

66

They all sat quietly for awhile thinking, then the bartender walked in and said, "Sagus, man in suit asking for Sagus."

"Huuh . . . what man?"

"Don't know man's name Sagus."

"Is he still here?"

"Si amigo."

Sagus smiled and said, "Gracias amigo," and the bartender left. He then said to his friends, "Well, are you guys gonna help me or not?"

"Yeah," replied Huck as Ed nodded, "What do you want us to do?"

Pointing in the direction of the back door, Sagus said, "Go out that door and come in the front. Order a couple beers, and when that fucking mole leaves, one of you follow him. I have to go somewhere and I'll be back in about an hour."

"I'll follow him," said Ed as he walked toward the back door.

"I guess I'll hang out in the bar until Ed comes back," replied Huck

"Okay," said Sagus, "and don't worry about buying beer. Before I leave I'll inform the bartender that you guys can drink on my tab."

While Huck sat in the bar drinking, Ed followed the mole as he went from bar to bar asking for Sagus. Finally the mole turned onto a back street, got into a car, and drove away. He couldn't follow the car, but he did get the license number, so on his way back to the bar he quietly summoned his friend, *"Hey Bobby . . ."*

"Yeah, long time no hear."

"I know, but now I'm hoping that our anthropomorphic abilities can be of help."

"Help with what?" replied Bobby.

67

Ed explained where they were and why, and what he and Huck had agreed to with Sagus.

Then Bobby said, *"Hey, I have a friend in the Confederacy that knows a CBI agent."*

"What are you talking about? What Confederacy? ..and what's a CBI agent?"

"The Confederate States of America, stupid, our sister country."

"What sister country?" queried Ed, *"You're not making any sense."*

"Wow!" Bobby exclaimed, *"Evidently, your existence has a different history than mine."*

"Considering our situation, Bobby, that makes sense. You see, the history books in my world tells us that there was a war in 1861 that lasted four years between the north and the south, and the north won. That war is commonly referred to as the Civil War or the War Between the States. The only CSA or Confederacy in our history only lasted four years, then we were one country again.

"I'm no history buff," replied Bobby, *"But I do know that it was around that time when the country split."*

"Well, history lessons aside, your friend in the Confederate Bureau of Investigation can't do me any good unless he knows how to appear in multiple universes."

"You're probably right," replied Bobby, *"but what a revelation about our respective histories?"*

"Yeah, that really is fascinating, but right now I need to get back. I'll be in touch."

"Okay, later."

When Ed returned to the bar, he and Huck met with Sagus in the office where Ed explained how the man in the suit went around to several bars asking for Sagus.

"Huuh. . ." said Sagus with a puzzled look on his face, "That tells me that they've found out that I'm working out of a bar, but they don't know which one."

Meanwhile, Bobby learned from his grandmother that anthros have the ability to view what's going on in parallel universes. This can be accomplished in a dream state by thinking of a location prior to going to sleep at night. Communication with mortals isn't possible–just viewing them is, similar to watching television. It had to be at night because, like most people, anthros can't usually go to sleep at will during the day. All Bobby needed to do was practice. Since time could be an important factor with what Ed and Huck were doing to help Sagus, Bobby initiated another contact: *"Hey Ed!"*

Ed got up from the crab couch and said, "I'll be right back, I gotta piss." When he got into the rest room, he answered, *"Yeah Bobby, what's up?"*

"I think I can be of help to Sagus."

"How's that?"

Bobby replied by explaining what his grandmother told him, then added, *"I'm going to try it tonight just for practice."*

"Why not practice on that guy I followed?" suggested Ed.

"That would be a good idea if I knew where he was."

"Maybe your friend in the Confederacy could find him for you with a license number."

"Good for you," said Bobby, *"you was able to get it before he drove off?"*

"Yeah, I didn't know what else to do at the moment. I certainly couldn't follow him."

"Okay, I'll see what I can do tonight and contact you tomorrow sometime."

"Later then."

69

When Ed returned to the crab couch, Huck said, "It looks like we're establishing residence in Tijuana."

"What do ya mean?" asked Ed.

"Sagus got us a room."

"It's not the Ritz," added Sagus, "it's not even the Holiday Inn, but it's a place to sleep."

"Do we get room service too?" asked Ed jokingly.

But Sagus just looked at him and answered with his customary, "Huuh."

Just before dawn the following morning, Ed heard Bobby summoning him and replied with a sleepy, *"What?"*

"Wake up sleepy head, I have something for ya."

After an exaggerated yawn and stretch, Ed looked at the ceiling and silently responded: *"What?"*

"Grandma was right," replied Bobby excitedly, *"in my mind's eye I was able to view the guy you followed."*

Wide awake now, Ed asked, *"If it works anything like what's happening between you and me, wouldn't you need to picture him in your mind?"*

"Didn't have to. Fortunately, that counterfeiting operation is going on in my existence as it is in yours. You see, I had my friend in the Confederacy get the address that's associated with the license number you gave me. When I went there, which was in San Diego, I saw the car, so I waited, and after a boring hour or so, I saw a man get into that car. Now," asked Bobby, *"I need to know if it's the same guy that you followed, so can you describe him to me?"*

"Yeah, he was around six feet tall with dark brown hair with a mustache and goatee. Oh, and I'd say he's about 35 or 40 and heavy set. Was that who you saw get into the car?"

"Yep, that's him. No bout a doubt it," replied Ed happily,

"Wow, I wonder what else, if anything, we're capable of doing that normal people can't?"

"We should probably get practiced with our present abilities before we start looking for more," suggested Bobby.

"I agree, in fact I better start practicing what you've just done," replied Ed, *"and I think I'll start with the same man."*

* * * *

The time had come for Ed to pick up his car. When he and Huck parked behind the bar, they honked the horn. A few seconds later, Sagus came out, looked inside and said, "Nice job. Tijuana might not be good for much, but they've been successful with the nice upholstery jobs they do."

"Good thing they do," said Huck as he got out of the car, "because from what Ed just told me, I think your little problem with your competitor just might be resolved."

As the three of them started toward the door that Sagus just came out of, Sagus put his arm around Ed's shoulder and said, "Is that right? Huuh . . . well, let's have a beer while you tell me about it."

After they all sat down in Sagus' office, Ed looked over at Huck and said to Sagus, "Huck jumped the gun by telling you that. It's not resolved yet, but he was right by saying that 'it might be.'

"You work fast, Ed," Sagus said with a quizzical look on his face, "You guys just got here yesterday. How in the hell . . .?"

Ed cut him off by saying, "When I followed the guy in the suit, I got his license number when he was done asking for you in bars. Then Ed made up a lie: "I then went to a pay phone and called a friend in Barstow who knows an FBI agent in San Diego. My friend in Barstow said he'd let me know if or when there was arrests."

"Huuh . . . how would you guys like a job working for me?" asked Sagus, "I could use people I trust, which is a little hard to find down here."

"Not me," replied Ed with another lie, "I've already got a job in Barstow. Besides that, my mom depends on me for things she's unable to do nowadays."

Without saying anything, Sagus looked over at Huck who also replied with a lie, "Thanks for the offer, but I must decline too. I also have a job, and a girlfriend, too."

"One of us will call you as soon as we hear whether your competition is out of the way or not," added Ed.

They hung around with Sagus for the rest of the day drinking and getting high, slept another night in their room, and left for home the next morning. They stopped off in San Diego and called the FBI office and dropped a dime on Sagus' competitor. As it turned out, they knew who the counterfeiters were, but didn't know where their operation was. The agent Huck talked to promised to call him when the arrest was made. About a week later, Huck got a letter in the mail from San Diego instead of a phone call. In it was the front page news in San Diego about a counterfeiting ring being taken into custody, along with all the paraphernalia needed in addition to the printing press. Huck gave Ed the front page newspaper article and called Sagus and told him to get a copy of the San Diego newspaper. Fortunately, all of this was successful in both universes.

CHAPTER SIX

Las Vegas

E d was in bed on this winter morning in January of 1967, wondering about his life in *this* universe as opposed to what it's like in other parallel universes. If there are copies of ourselves in hundreds, thousands, or even millions of other universes, the possibilities, experiences, and abilities are no doubt too monumental to even try to imagine.

He was also feeling guilt over the part he and Huck played in Tijuana helping Sagus. Using his anthropomorphic abilities to abet criminal activity made him uncomfortable. Cutting his reverie short by bringing his mind back to the present, he wondered what he should do with the day that lay before him. When he entered the living room, he greeted his mother by saying, "Top of the mornin' to ya, mom." Ed's jovial mood was interrupted when he read the sadness on his mother's face. "What's the matter, mom?" he asked, not knowing what to expect.

"Sit down, baby, I have to talk to you."

"De ja vu," Ed thought as he sat down on the couch, preparing himself for whatever was to come. Ed then spontaneously looked outside to see if his dad's car was there. It wasn't. As he turned back towards his mother, he asked, "Something has happened to dad, hasn't it?"

She was unable to answer him, because she immediately began to weep. Ed's first thoughts weren't for himself, but how he could comfort his mother, so he went over and took her in his arms. Ed loved his parents, but right then his mother needed him. He didn't focus on the loss of the best possible father that a son could ever hope to have until later.

After a few minutes, Mrs. Smith started gaining control and said, "I'll be okay now Honey, thank you, I've been holding it in since I found out. I even told myself that I wouldn't cry when I saw you."

Mr. Smith had been involved in a car accident with a drunk driver. Ed and his mother talked about that and agreed that drunk drivers were a fact of life. Both of them admitted that they'd both been guilty of it themselves. Fortunately, Mr. Smith didn't have to suffer–death was instantaneous.

After Ed consoled his mother and talked about the funeral and all the other rituals that come with death, Mrs. Smith told her son that she wanted to be alone for a while, and was going to her room to lie down.

After breakfast, his head was still spinning. However, he did feel somewhat good about himself for being able to contain himself as he comforted his mother. Once he placed his dirty dishes in the sink, he went back to his room and started listening to records. After each 45 played, another would drop onto the turntable, until the stack of records had played out. Ed then sat in silence, thinking about the abilities he possessed that most people didn't have. With these thought in mind, he summoned his friend.

"Bobby . . ."

"Yeah," replied Bobby, *"hey, I'm sorry about your dad. He was a good man."*

"You know what? I can't remember ever telling my dad that I loved him."

"That doesn't mean that you didn't."

"No, it doesn't."

"Then don't worry about it, Ed. Love isn't something that comes from the mouth–it comes from the heart."

Ed pondered on that momentarily and replied, *"Thanks, Bobby, I needed to hear that, but there's something else I'd like to know."*

"You'd like to know if you can communicate with your dad, right?"

"Well, wouldn't you want to talk to your parents if one of them died?" asked Ed.

"Probably, but as you know, we can only communicate with other anthros." Being caught in traffic while this conversation was going on, Bobby then said, *"I gotta go, some ass-hole in another car is pissed off at me for sitting at this red light too long. Later, ole buddy.*

Ed sat in his room for a few minutes lost in thought, then walked into the main part of the house and told his mom he was going for a ride.

Ed got into his car and started driving aimlessly. He'd been cruising around for about ten minutes, when he decided to buy himself a couple of beers. He parked in front of a liquor store, and just as he was getting out of his car, he saw his friend and said, "Hey Jimbo*!"*

"Hey, Ed!" Jimbo replied, "What'cha up to*?"*

"Nothin' much, just gettin' a couple beers and going for a ride."

"I'll go with ya," Jimmy replied, "just let me lock up my brother's car."

When they left the liquor store, Jimbo reached over and turned down the radio and asked, "Wanna go to Las Vegas? I've got some money that's burnin a hole in my pocket."

"I don't know," replied Ed "My dad just died. I probably shouldn't leave my mother right now."

"Oh no, when did this happen?" Jimbo asked, genuinely concerned.

75

"Yesterday," Ed replied somberly as he pulled into a gas station and parked next to a phone booth, "But hold on a minute. I'm going to call my mom. Las Vegas sounds like fun, and I can damn sure use some fun right now."

When Ed returned from making his phone call, he started the engine and put it in gear as he looked at Jimbo and said, "I told her about seeing you, and what you suggested, and she told me to, by all means, go! She said she'd be fine, and that she'd rather take care of the funeral arrangements herself anyway, and would let me know where and when the service was on."

After they gassed up and got on the freeway, Ed wanted to confide to his friend about his abilities as an anthropomorphic, but decided against it, realizing that it would be too outlandish for anyone to believe.

As they were passing Baker, they reminisced about their trip to Ash Meadows, then Jimbo asked, "Have you ever been to Las Vegas?

"Once. My parents took me and Bobby up there with them for a weekend when we were about 13 or 14. Have you?"

"No."

They continued their conversation as they drew closer to their destination. Fortunately, the traffic was light and the weather was nice. It was about two o'clock in the afternoon when they pulled onto Las Vegas Boulevard. As they drove down the strip, they passed the Hacienda on the left, and then the Aladdin on the right. The first intersection they approached was Tropicana. When the light turned green, Ed asked, "You wanna see Boulder Dam?"

"Why go see an old dam?"

"An old dam?" Ed repeated quizzically, "This old dam is really big. It has enough concrete in it to pave a two lane highway from here to New York City."

"New York City?" Jimbo asked incredulously, "You mean

Salt Lake City, don't you?"

"No, New York City."

"Wow, that's a lot of fucking concrete," agreed Jimbo, "Okay, let's check it out."

They pased through east Las Vegas and then Henderson, and were approaching Boulder City, when Ed said, "Let's get more beer."

"Okay with me. Pull into that Stop n Go over there, and I'll run in and get it."

When they got to the dam, they parked on the Nevada side. For the time being they stayed in the car drinking beer, smoking cigarettes and talking. They were in no hurry, and were enjoying themselves—especially Ed, because it took his mind off of his father's death. By this time it was around three o'clock, and while they were sitting there, they saw an old red Dodge pick-up with a camper shell on it stop on the dam. The passenger in the pick-up got out and approached a man standing on the sidewalk opposite the dam looking at Lake Mead. The man from the truck put his arm around the man's neck and put a rag to his face. When the man went limp, the driver of the old truck pulled up, got out and helped put the limp body in back of the truck. The passenger of the truck got into the camper shell with the man who was obviously being kidnapped, and then they drove away. All this happened in a couple minutes.

Amazed at what they'd just witnessed, Ed and Jimbo just looked at each other. Then Ed asked, "What do you think about that?"

"Wow! I've only seen shit like that in movies."

As they watched the truck drive away, Ed started his car and said, "I'm gonna follow them."

"Why?" Jimbo asked, "We could get ourselves killed fuckin around with the mafia."

"I don't think the mafia drives around in old pick-ups like

77

that," replied Ed now starting to slur his words, "I'm just going to discreetly follow them."

What Jimbo didn't know, was that Ed was experiencing an anthropomorphic phenomenon. Ed wasn't following the truck out of mere curiosity or adventure, but rather a driving force that was out of his control.

When the old pick-up was on the other side of the dam, it made a U-turn and started back across the dam again. When Ed got to the other side of the dam, he parked again and said, "If I follow them back across the dam, they might notice that I'm following them."

"Yeah, but why follow em?" asked Jimbo starting to slur his words too, "What the fuck can you do?"

"Well," Ed replied, saying anything to keep Jimbo from discouraging him, "I think I know the guy that was kidnapped, and I...."

Jimbo interrupted by saying, "Bullshit! You're just fuckin nosy."

Ed had to admit to himself that he really didn't know why he was doing this, but he felt a strong compulsion to somehow get the kidnapped man's attention, but he didn't want to put him and Jimbo's life in danger doing it. Perhaps it was a mafia thing, Ed thought, but after a few minutes he threw caution to the wind and said, "I bet that truck is going back into Vegas. I'm gonna catch up to em and lag behind far enough to keep them from noticing us."

"Whatever, you're the one that's driving, but I didn't even get to see this bad-ass dam that has so much concrete in it."

"Relax and have another beer. We can always come back."

"We can't if the mafia kills us."

"Hey man, where's your sense of adventure?"

"Adventure hell. Stupidity!"

They were on the west side of Henderson before they caught sight of the old pick up. "There they are, Jimbo. They just pulled up to that bar."

"They're probably like us and wanna get more beer," replied Jimbo, still trying to discourage Ed.

The kidnappers went into the pub leaving their captive in the truck.

Ed parked a short distance from the bar and walked to where the truck was parked. Fortunately the truck was in a position for Ed to peer inside the camper shell. When he got back in the car and started the motor, he had a perplexed expression on his face. Then Jimbo asked, "What's wrong, Dick Tracy?"

"He ain't in there."

"Good," replied Jimbo, obviously relieved, "I'm glad; now can we go back and see this bad-ass dam?"

They returned to the dam and luckily got their previous parking place. Then they walked over to peer down at the massive-sized dam.

"Wow!" exclaimed Jimbo, "How would you like me to throw you off of this dam?"

They finally decided they were getting too drunk to be driving around, so they went back to East Las Vegas, rented a room, and passed out. About two O'clock in the morning, Jimbo awoke and tried to awaken Ed, but he was out cold. So Jimbo took a shower and cleaned up. Before he left, he placed a fifty dollar bill on the dresser.

About eight o'clock in the morning, Ed finally awoke. He looked around and didn't see his traveling partner. As he arose and started toward the rest room, he noticed the money on the dresser, and a note that read:

Ed,

Tried to get you up, but you wouldn't budge. I couldn't

stay cooped up in this room waiting for you to wake up. I
paid for another night. Meet you back here.

   Jimbo

   As Ed was taking a shower, he thought it would be a good
time to go back to the dam, just in case. Since Jimbo was out
whoring around, he wouldn't have to put up with his whining
about the mafia.

   Ed left the motel room and went to a casino and had one of
their bargain breakfasts. As he was leaving the casino, he
couldn't resist patronizing the local one-arm bandits. What was
only intended to be a few coins on the way out, turned into two
hours, however, and he'd managed to come out even. He left
content that he had played for two hours on their money, and
was provided free beer for the duration.

   Ed parked a short distance from where he and Jimbo were the
day before. The road to the dam is on a steep winding hill or
mountain, but there are rest spot clearings on the road
periodically. Ed parked on the last one before the dam.

   He locked his car and walked down to the sidewalk on the
dam like many tourists do. As he started strolling down the
sidewalk, directly in front of him, he saw something that set him
aback. The very man that was kidnapped was standing there
gazing out over Lake Mead. As Ed approached, he noticed that
the man kept looking at the clock on the Nevada side of the
dam, which read eleven o'clock.

   For lack of better words, Ed walked up to the man and asked,
"Do you have the time, sir?"

   The man looked at Ed, looked at the clock, then back at Ed,
and with a wrinkled forehead, he replied, "Eleven o'clock."

   Ed acted as though he wasn't aware that the clock was there,
and then said, "Oh! I didn't notice that clock up there." Then he
turned his head in the other direction and pretended to notice the
clock was on the Arizona side, and then said, "This must be

where the time changes, because the clock over there says twelve o'clock."

As soon as the word twelve was out of Ed's mouth, the man's facial expression changed into that of confusion, and then he asked, "Did you just say twelve o'clock?"

It wasn't the time of twelve o'clock that alarmed the man; it was Ed saying the word twelve. At that instant, the man turned towards Ed, still looking confused, and suddenly walked off.

Ed then realized that he was receiving distorted telepathic signals from this man, but was unsure how to deal with it. His natural instinct was to make an effort to help, so he followed the guy and tried saying something silently: *Can you hear me? If you can, please stop, turn around, and look into my eyes.*

The man stopped, turned around, and looked at Ed with a strange look that could only be described as fear.

The two men held eye contact momentarily, and then Ed silently said, *"You appear to be unsure of what is happening between us right now. Is that true?"*

Without uttering a word, the man silently replied, *"Yeah, it damn sure is."*

This is when Ed offered his hand, smiled, and said aloud, "Hi, my name is Ed Smith."

The man reluctantly accepted Ed's hand as his expression began to relax, and replied, "Hi, I'm Jim Matthews, but I go by Herby."

Before Herby had a chance to say anything else, Ed said, "You look like a man that could use a beer."

"Yeah, I damn sure could." replied Herby, still unsure of what was happening.

Every time Ed offered a congenial smile, and/or a little amiable conversation, Herby relaxed a little more.

"Well, let's go to my car, I just happen to have some."

As they walked in single file up the narrow sidewalk, Ed said over his shoulder, "The beer won't be very cold because it's been in my car all night, but I don't think either of us is going to bitch about that under the circumstances."

As they stepped off the sidewalk and started toward Ed's car, Herby replied, "You got that right!"

When they arrived at the car, Ed unlocked the doors, and they got in. He grabbed a six-pack container with four beers in it from the back seat and handed one to Herby."

"Thanks," Herby said hesitatingly, "What was your name again?"

"Ed."

"Well, I hope you can answer some questions for me."

"I'll make you a deal, Herby," replied Ed as he opened a beer, "I'll answer your questions, if you'll answer mine, and you can go first. How's that?"

After he took a big drink of his beer, Herby took a deep breath, closed his eyes, laid his head back, and then exhaled. He remained that way momentarily, then he raised his head, looked out of the passenger side window, and silently said, *"I'm doing this to make sure that it did, and is now really happening."*

"Yeah, it's definitely happening," Ed responded quietly.

"Good," Herby replied audibly, "then I don't belong in the funny farm."

"No," Ed said questioningly, "why would you think that?"

"You see," explained Herby, "it isn't just this telepathy between us, or the other phenomenon that I've experienced that has me so confused."

As Herby was talking, Ed took a drink of his beer and started to say something, but before he could, Herby raised his finger and said, "So, prior to seeing me on the dam a while ago, have you ever seen me before, and if you have, have you seen anyone

82

with me?"

"Yes to both questions." Ed's reply got Herby's undivided attention, and he started to say something, but Ed cut him short and said, "But first, explain how you're unclear, and maybe I can clear it up for you."

"Okay, but I think I should explain my present dilemma. When you found me awhile ago, I had no idea how long I'd been standing there; in fact, I wasn't aware of anything until you told me that it was twelve o'clock. The last thing I remember prior to that, was standing on the dam, but not in the same place where you found me."

"I can explain that, Herby. Yesterday, a friend of mine and I witnessed you being kidnapped," then Ed described where on the dam this happened.

"Really?"

"Yeah. At the time, my friend said, 'Wow! I've only seen that kind of shit in the movies.'"

"That explains it then," replied Herby, starting to loosen up a little, "You see, this isn't the first time this has happened, but before I attributed it to the other shit that's been happening to me lately. So, you can see why I was so confused?"

"Yeah, I do, no wonder you thought you might be losing it, so I better explain a few things to you, but you're gonna to have to trust me."

"I don't have any other choice, Ed."

When Herby said that, Ed thought back to how many times he'd said similar things to Bobby.

They ran out of beer and wanted more, so they went to Boulder City and got some, and then went to Ed's motel room to continue their conversation.

When they entered the room, Ed found another note from Jimbo that read:

83

Ed,

Don't seem like we're gonna ever catch up with each other, so I'll see you back in Barstow. If I don't see you before, I'll try to get over for your Dad's funeral.

Jimbo

"Looks like my partner split back to Barstow," Ed said as he tossed the note so Herby could read it, "Just as well. With him around, we would've had a lot of explaining to do, and we would've had to communicate silently, and carry on regular conversations with him at the same time."

Ed explained how he came to be in the Las Vegas area with Jimbo, then Herby explained his domestic situation. They talked about their telepathic abilities and their mutual experiences with them. During this conversation Ed gave Herby a word to add to his vocabulary.

"Anthropomorphic?" Herby asked after lighting a cigarette, "I thought that meant people thinking things like their dog smiling at them."

"It does mean that," replied Ed, as he too lit a cigarette, "When I looked up the word in the dictionary, I found that the word can be interpreted different ways, as a lot of words in the English language do. However, in an unabridged dictionary I found in the library, one of the definitions of anthropomorphic included the word supernaturalism and something about the universe. Whatever all that means, well . . . I don't know Herby, it's pretty far out stuff."

After continuing their conversation quietly for an hour or so, Herby said out loud, "You know what? I've had about all I can handle for one day, so I bet...."

Ed interrupted, "Why don't you kick back here for awhile? I'll go play the slot machines or something."

Herby thought about it momentarily and asked, "Can I use the phone? I better keep the peace at home, even though there hasn't really been any real peace for a long time."

"Yeah, go for it."

Herby called home and made up a believable story that wasn't really a lie, and when he hung up the phone, he said, "Okay, I'm gonna crash for awhile. Would you wake me up in about four or five hours?"

"Sure," replied Ed, "it's four o'clock now, so I'll be back around nine or ten to wake you."

"Okay, do you need any money?"

"No, my partner left me enough, but thanks for asking."

So Ed went to play the slots and check out the town. When he wasn't busy playing the slots or thinking about Herby and everything that had happened recently, he was thinking about his poor mother. He asked himself if he was being selfish leaving her there to grieve by herself? With that thought in mind, he found a pay phone.

"Hello."

"Hi Mom," greeted Ed as cheerfully as possible.

"Hi, baby. Are you having a good time?"

"Yeah, it's an interesting place alright, so much so, that Jimbo and I lost each other. He took a bus back to Barstow. Are you doing okay mom? How are the funeral arrangements going? I'll come back right now if you want me to?"

"No honey, you stay there for now. It will be at least another couple of days before the service. Just call me again tomorrow so I won't worry about you."

"Okay mom, I love you."

It was about midnight before Ed finally realized what time it was. He went to the cashier's cage and turned in his cup full of coins, and was happy to find that he was ten dollars richer.

When he entered the room, he slammed the door, and in

doing so, he saw Herby open his eyes.

"Oh, I'm sorry, I didn't mean to wake you up," Ed said, as if slamming the door was an accident.

"*Liar*," Herby quietly replied, holding eye contact momentarily.

With a smile, Ed replied aloud, "Hey, all this can be fun."

"Yeah, we might as well make the best of it," added Herby.

They made small talk for awhile, and then Ed asked, "Why do you think you can't remember anything that happened to you during the time you were kidnapped, Herby?"

"I don't know. I can't even remember being kidnapped."

"It was probably because the guy that first grabbed you put a rag over your mouth. It was probably laced with a drug of some kind."

"Yeah," Herby replied with a bewildered look on his face, "Now that you mention it, I do have a vague memory of something smelling funny."

"I wonder if you would've remembered that, if I hadn't mentioned it."

"Probably not," agreed Herby, "and I wouldn't have known I was kidnapped either if you hadn't saw it happen and told me about it. I wonder what the fuck's going on, anyway?"

"You've been drugged, and possibly even hypnotized."

"I wonder why though, and I...." Herby didn't finish what he started to say, and then appeared to be in deep thought momentarily, and then he asked, "You know what, Ed?"

"What."

"I haven't told anybody about what's been happening to me lately, but under the circumstances . . . you see, I'm not happily married. I am married, but we're just going through the motions for the kids' sake. Anyway, I have this girlfriend, and her dad

86

owns and operates a Sports Book out on the strip."

"What's a Sports Book?"

"It's where you bet on horse races, fights, baseball and football, and so on. It's part of the gaming industry, and if you've heard much about gaming in Nevada, then you've probably heard about the ties that organized crime has with it."

"You mean the mafia?"

"Yeah, but it's not the way it's portrayed in the movies. Plus, I heard that it insults them when they're referred to as the mafia. It's not like the Al Capone or Mickey Cohen days with machine guns and all that crap. It's all about business and big money shit. Anyway, Trip's dad is involved in all that."

"Who's Trip?

"My girlfriend. Her real name is Teri Galloway."

"And you've been telling her about your experiences?"

"Yeah," replied Herby, as he started pacing around the room, "but only with her.. ..and nothing about parallel universes. Telling my wife about any of it would only get me committed to the funny farm."

"Hmmm."

They kept talking along those lines until they were convinced that Trip's father was at the bottom of Herby's kidnapping.

CHAPTER SEVEN

Herby

Back at home in Barstow, Ed was in bed thinking about his anthropomorphic counterpart in Las Vegas while listening to Fats Domino sing *Walking to New Orleans*. He learned that there were people in Las Vegas of unsavory character who'd like to manipulate anthros for their benefit.

Ed's guilty conscience about leaving his mom in grief over the death of her husband brought him back home before he was done in Vegas. His business in Nevada was really more important than the emotional ties with his mother. After all, her broken heart and sense of loss would eventually heal, and so would his. But at least he'd made it back for his dad's funeral – and he knew that was important for his mother.

Ed got out of bed when the last forty five played out, and then he went into the living room where his mother was sitting.

"Hi mom."

"Good morning, baby. Did you have a good time in Las Vegas?"

"I did," Ed replied as he was taking his customary seat on the sofa, "How have you been?"

"Oh, better I guess," she replied, which really wasn't true, and then added, "I've been trying to stay busy, but it's hard not to think."

"Me too, mom, so I'm going back to Vegas. I really only came back to check on you. When you told me on the phone that you were okay, that suggested to me that you were just saying that so I wouldn't worry about you."

She ignored his concern and asked, "What did you do, find a girlfriend there?"

Ed felt like saying yes to that question, because it would've been easier to lie, but instead he said, "No, but I did meet a guy who's going to take me to all the fun spots. He says that it's not too expensive if you know how to do it and where to go." Ed was made uncomfortable by the way his mom was looking at him, so he said, "You work a lot which keeps you from thinking, and that's a good way to cope. Well, staying busy in Vegas with my new friend is my way of coping."

"You're probably right, so go back to Las Vegas and do what you have to do to get through this, and I'll do what I have to do here. Everybody has their own way of coping, I suppose. Just call me if you're going to be there very long, okay?"

"Okay, mom."

By ten o'clock that morning Ed was en-route back to Las Vegas. He'd picked up a couple six packs of beer, and was listening to Otis Redding sing, *I've Been Loving You Too Long*, on the radio.

He was going about eighty five with the radio turned up so loud that he couldn't hear the car behind him honking his horn. One of his rear wheels was wobbling, and when it came off, Ed's car went off the road and rolled several times before landing upside down.

* * * *

Herby went to work the next day expecting a call from Ed around two or three o'clock, but when it was quitting time, and not a word from Ed, he went home and forgot about it.

Mrs. Smith was sitting solemnly in the emergency room at Barstow Hospital. First her husband; and now her only child had been on the operating table for three hours. The longer it took, the more convinced she was that she'd never see him again.

90

An hour later, a haggard looking surgeon entered the waiting room and said, "Your son is alive Mrs. Smith, but at this time, I don't know if he's going to make it or not. I'm sure you can understand why I hate this part of my job."

Mrs. Smith understood the surgeon's obvious discomfort, so she came to his rescue with a weak smile and replied, "Thank you doctor, I don't envy any part of your job."

"There are times when it's rewarding."

"Thanks for trying, doctor. I guess I'll go home now and wait for my son to wake up. Will you call me when he gains consciousness?"

"Yes ma'am. It may not be me who calls, but you'll be the first to know."

The accident took place approximately ten miles north of Baker, not quite half way to Las Vegas from Barstow.

Every day for a week Ed's friends came to the hospital to visit, but he was still in a coma. Two weeks later, nothing had changed.

Since the day that Mrs. Smith walked out of the emergency room, she'd not looked back. She didn't call either, preferring to wait for the inevitable phone call.

* * *

It was Sunday morning and Herby was at home asleep in a chair. Again he'd left Trip in a motel room. He'd made it home around his customary time of six o'clock. During this time together, he hadn't bothered telling her anything about what he'd been going through.

He wanted to wait until he heard from Ed before making any decisions. He was simply too new at this to take an initiative. Their conflict with organized crime was to be a joint effort.

About eight o'clock, still in his chair in the living room,

Herby's kids were up and making noise. He could hear the sizzle of bacon frying but it was the smell of it that aroused his attention. Just before opening his eyes, his wife shook him and asked, "Why don't you get in bed, honey?"

"Uh, yeah okay," and he went back to the bedroom. Just as he was about to doze off, he heard a familiar voice, so he silently responded, *"Hey Ed, it's about time I heard from you."*

"Yeah, I know, but there's a good reason. Right now as you hear me in your head, I'm unconscious in the Barstow Hospital in a coma."

"What!"

"Yeah, on the way back up there yesterday, I was involved in a car accident."

"Are you telling me that you can still do this while you're in a coma?"

"Yeah, believe it or not, I can, but I can't seem to regain consciousness."

"Wow!" replied Herby, now wide awake, *"we still had a lot to do, and I still have questions."*

"I know, but something tells me that this probably happened to me for a reason. Anyway, you're right, we didn't get to talk enough, but there's always gonna be questions. I still have a lot of them too, but we're both gonna have to be patient. Uh . . . shit, I'm starting to feel weak, Herby, we're gonna have to talk later."

"Okay, get well Ed"

Having said that out loud, it caught Martha's attention as she was walking by the bedroom door. When she opened it, she asked, "Did you say something, honey?"

"No, just talkin' to myself. I even woke myself up," he responded instinctively.

She looked at him weird-like, then closed the door.

Herby got dressed, had breakfast, and went outside to work in the yard.

* * * *

It was the 3rd of July, 1967, three months since losing her husband and then getting the shocking news of Ed's accident, but Mrs. Smith never gave up hope. As long as she didn't receive a phone call from the hospital saying otherwise, she knew that her son was still alive. However, when Ed didn't regain consciousness after three weeks, they called to inform her that he'd been transferred to the County Hospital in San Bernardino.

As she was doing house work one day, the telephone rang. Over the months she'd learned how to control her anxiety when the phone rang.

"Hello."

"Mrs. Smith?"

"Yes."

"This is the County Hospital in San Bernardino, and I'd like to inform you that your son has regained consciousness and asking for you."

"Oh God, thank you," she replied excitedly, "would you tell him that I'll be there as soon as I can?"

"Of course, Mrs Smith, I know this must be a happy moment for you. He actually came to yesterday, but we've been observing him for the last twenty-four hours. So far, he's doing fine. We still have a few more tests to run, and then we'll know more."

"Okay, and thanks again."

"You're welcome, and please drive carefully."

Mrs. Smith hung up the phone and released three months of suppressed tears. Tears of happiness and relief.

The young nurse that stood at Ed's bedside asked, "How do you feel, Mr. Smith?"

"I don't know, I can't really tell."

"That's good," she replied with a smile.

When she started fiddling with the EEG, he asked, "What are you doing?"

"Do you know what this machine is?"

"No."

"It's an electroencephalogram—EEG for short. It traces the electrical activity of the brain and records it on the electroencephalograph," she said pointing at the graph.

Ed was admiring the pretty nurse as she hooked him up to the EEG. While making the final adjustments, she said, "Mr. Smith…"

He cut her off by saying, "Call me Ed, I hate that mister shit."

"Alright Ed," she replied with a smile, "When I turn this machine on, I want you to lie perfectly still. Don't make any rapid eye movements, or don't move your tongue or grit your teeth, and above all don't talk. Just lie there as still as you can, okay?"

Ed smiled, nodded his head and said, "Maybe I should close my eyes too, because some things I can't control when I'm looking at something I like."

She smiled but didn't respond.

When Ed started to say something, she gestured with her finger over her lips for him to be quiet, then turned on the machine. She took a minute or so to make the necessary adjustments and appeared to be satisfied with them when she said, "Move your eyes to the left, and then to the right, then back and forth a couple times."

Ed complied and waited for further instructions.

"Everything looks good," she said smiling, then added, "I think you're ready to visit with your mother now."

Ed's eyes widened and then he asked, "Is she here?"

"Not yet, but she's on her way, but before she gets here, I think there is something you should know."

"Oh, no," he replied, turning his head, "you're married?"

At first she thought she'd upset him, but then realized he was messing with her. "I'm serious now. There's something that you need to know," she said, forcing seriousness.

"What then?" he asked suspiciously.

"You have been in a coma for the past three months. Today is the third of July."

Ed looked at her with questioning eyes, trying to determine whether she was joking or not. Finally he asked, "Can I see a newspaper?" They held eye contact momentarily, and then he added, "It's not that I don't believe you, I just . . ."

She interrupted with a hand gesture and said, "I know, Ed, say no more, I'll go and get one for you. I wasn't thinking right, I should've had one here for you in the first place."

As she exited the room, Ed thought to himself, "*I know that I've been in a coma, but just now, spontaneously, I behaved as though I didn't know. What's strange is the way I know. Weird-like, kind of like I'm two people or something.*"

Because of the indistinctness of the English language, Ed struggled with articulating what was going on in his head. When thinking, people naturally think in their native tongue, which is generally only one language. In this country the language is English. Ed was trying to understand his spontaneous response to the nurse, and his form of consciousness.

The nurse returned with a newspaper, and Ed caught himself impatiently grabbing it out of her hands and hungrily reading the date on it. Again he felt that previous phenomenon, knowing full well what was happening, yet behaving as though he didn't. Rather than continue analyzing it, he allowed his intuition to lead him wherever he was destined to go.

When Ed looked up from the paper, he held eye contact with the nurse momentarily and then he smiled and asked, "Does this mean I have to stay awake for three months so it'll come out even?"

"Yeah, right, silly," she replied with gentle sarcasm, then said, "Rest that active mind of yours for now, I have some other patients to attend to."

He managed to doze off for awhile, but when he woke up, Mrs. Smith was by his side. They made small talk for awhile, and then he asked, "I wonder how soon I can go home?"

"I talked to your doctor before I came in here, and he said that would depend on whether there are facilities in Barstow for physical therapy."

"Physical therapy, what's that?"

"You have to go through some vigorous exercising in order to restore your strength, honey."

Ed understood when his legs buckled trying to make it to the rest room. "Oh shit, I see what you mean. When will we know whether Barstow has facilities or not?"

"I'll find out when I talk to the doctor."

"Okay mom."

Not long after that, when the food cart arrived, Mrs. Smith said, "While you're eating I'll go see if I can find out anything."

Ed would go home the following morning. Barstow Hospital had a physical therapy room.

* * * *

96

During Ed's hospitalization, Herby had a couple minor anthropomorphic experiences. Occasionally, he'd consult with Ed on what he'd hoped to be a mentor basis. However, Ed wasn't being the help that Herby expected him to be, much like Bobby wasn't the help that Ed expected him to be when all this started.

Ed and Herby agreed not to act on Jerry Galloway - Trip's father. Herby told Ed that he hadn't mentioned anything to his girlfriend, Trip. They agreed that there was no sense in Herby complicating his relationship with Trip by asking her questions about her father. Besides, anything that she told her father about Herby wouldn't be said in malice or deception towards Herby.

Now that Herby was pretty sure it was either drugs or hypnosis, or both, that prevented him from remembering what occurred during those lapses of time, he'd hopefully be prepared mentally if it happened again.

Back in Barstow, Ed was eager to recover; therefore, every day he'd have his mother take him to physical therapy for exercise treatment. He also had to adhere to a stringent diet.

After five weeks of continual and increasingly rigorous exercise, Ed was almost back to normal. He wanted to get back to Vegas to his anthropomorphic counterpart, and attend to their issues with organized crime. He'd told his mother to keep his discharge from the hospital a secret. He didn't want to give any of his friends an opportunity to sidetrack him. There was one thing that happened naturally that made it easier for him to conceal his identity; he had three months growth of hair on his face.

Ed asked his mother if she'd buy him a cheap transportation car until he could get a job and pay her back. He explained his plan to move to Vegas where he wouldn't have to live around the pressure of his peers. He wanted to cut loose the drugs and alcohol.

A week later, Ed was on his way to Vegas in a reliable

transportation car that his mother got for him. As he was driving over Halloran Summit, he quietly asked, *"Hey Herby, is this a good time?"*

"Yeah, business is slow right now," Herby quietly replied. At the time he was working behind the parts counter of the local Lincoln-Mercury dealership.

"I'm on my way there now."

"About time," Herby replied silently as a customer walked up.

"Good morning, sir," said the customer.

Then Herby had to respond to the customer's greeting aloud: "Good morning, what can I help you with?"

Then Ed responded to Herby silently, *"Are you ready to fight the mafia?"*

As Ed asked that silently, the customer asked Herby a question. "Do you have an alternator for a 64 Ford Galaxie 500?"

"No," Herby replied to the customer, "we just sold the last one, but I can have one here for you tomorrow.

"Okay thanks," said the customer, "I'll be back around this time tomorrow."

As the customer was walking out, Herby said quietly, *"I can tell that I'm gonna have to talk to only one person at a time. This could get confusing."*

After they talked for awhile, Herby explained to Ed how to get to Friendly Fergies, and they agreed to meet there around six fifteen. Ed made it to the bar around five-thirty. As he walked in, the noise startled him. Friendly Fergies had an abundance of slot machines, with bells ringing everywhere. Whenever a machine hit a jack pot, a loud bell would start ringing. Fergies was a pretty big place for a bar. They even had a change girl and a slot mechanic on duty 24 hours. Ed didn't have much money to squander on the one-arm bandits, so he walked up to the bar and ordered a coke. He'd been there about a half hour when he saw his friend walk in the front door. Herby was standing there looking around the place, obviously searching for Ed. Ed then noticed, for the first time really, how strange Herby was. He was a couple inches taller than Ed, and was going prematurely bald. He also had this nervous twitch in his face that looked like exaggerated blinks of his eyes, which caused his head to jerk a little, and when he did all of this, he made a sucking noise with his tongue and teeth. All this was subtle. One needed to be around him for awhile before it became noticeable.

The large bar in Fergies was in an L shape, and had two bartenders. Ed was seated at the far part of the bar, observing Herby between slot machines. Finally he got his attention, waved, and said quietly, *"Over here where the bar turns, Herby."*

Herby smiled and started walking in that direction. As he got closer, he silently replied, *"There you are."*

When Herby took the seat next to Ed, they shook hands, and Ed asked aloud, "Want a beer or something?"

Ed had previously informed Herby that he was making an effort to stay clean and sober, so Herby said, "Yeah, I'll have a 7-up."

"So, how've you been?" asked Ed after taking a drink of his diet coke.

"I've been alright, but what about you? Have you recovered?" Herby asked sincerely.

"Yeah, I'm pretty much back to normal, but my greatest concern right now is finding a cheap place to live."

"Hmm . . ." pondered Herby, then he said, "Hey, I know a guy that needs a roommate. He used to work where I do in the service department as a mechanic, that is until he got fired for being stoned on the job."

"Well, that doesn't make em a bad guy. I can't count the jobs I lost because of that."

"Terry has a nice house, too, from his previous marriage. She just took the kids and split."

"Give him a call then. The sooner I'm settled, the better."

"Okay," Herby replied as he stood up and took some money out of his pocket. "Here, pay for the drinks while I go make the call."

Herby went outside to a phone booth.

"Hello."

"How's it going, Terry?"

"Good. How about you?"

"I'm alright. Just wanted to know if you're still looking for a roommate?"

"Yeah, wanna move in?"

"Fuck no! I wouldn't live with you, but a friend of mine will; that is, as long as I don't tell him how fucked up you get all the time."

"Hey, I don't get fucked up that much anymore."

"Whatever. Anyway, are you going to be home for awhile?"

"Yeah, bring em on over."

"Okay, see you in about a half hour."

Herby and Ed finished their soda's and went to Terry's house in Herby's car.

They pulled up in front of the house and parked. By the time they were out of the car, Terry had opened his front door and was standing there waiting for them. As they approached Terry asked, "Are you still a parts man, Herby?"

By the time they'd reached where Terry was standing, Herby replied, "Yeah, and what about you, are you working?"

"Yeah, out on the Boulder Highway in east Las Vegas, at a used car lot. I fix em, and they sell em."

"Ed, this is Terry Piles," said Herby, "and this is Ed Smith."

They shook hands and greeted each other, and then Terry said, "C'mon in, but you'll have to excuse the house. Ever since my ole lady left, I haven't done a good cleaning."

"You ain't going to either, if I know you," said Herby.

"Shhh. Don't tell Ed that until after he moves in."

"How do you know if you even want me to move in?" asked Ed.

"Although Herby can be an asshole sometimes, I do trust him, so if he says you're alright, I'll take his word for it."

They made a financial agreement and talked about living arrangements, and once they came to an understanding, Terry said, "Hey guys, I've gotta go to work. After I talked to you on the phone, Herby, my boss called and said they need me to R and R a transmission." Terry then turned to Ed and said, "Since you live here now, just make yourselves at home."

Terry left and that gave Ed and Herby a chance to talk. They had a lot of catching up to do.

"I think I mentioned that Boulder Dam wasn't the only time or place I woke up in that disoriented condition."

"Yeah, you did, but you didn't say much of anything about it."

"Well, I probably didn't mention that it happened at Fergies, and today is the first time I've been there since," Herby explained.

"No, you didn't mention anything like that."

Thinking out loud, Herby said, "I wonder if the bartender still works there that was there when I came to?" Then he looked at Ed and added, "I should've asked that question when we were

101

there."

"You could ask when you take me back to get my car."

"Yeah," replied Herby, "good idea."

"So you're sure your girlfriend's father is behind it, huh?"

"I'm pretty damn sure, Ed, but all I have is circumstantial evidence, and I don't want Trip involved in all of this. It's probably best that we make sure my suspicion is right."

On the way back to Fergies, Herby told Ed that when he went to work the next morning, he'd find out if they need any parts chasers, since Ed needed a job. After parking next to Ed's car at Fergies, they went in for a soda to see if they could find out anything. As they took a seat at the part of the bar that was closest to the door, the bartender walked up and asked, "What'll it be, gentlemen?"

"A couple of 7-up's, please," replied Herby as he reached for his wallet.

When the bartender returned with the drinks, they watched him take the money off the counter and waited for him to bring back the change before asking about the other bartender. When the bartender returned, Herby asked, "I wonder if you could tell me something?"

"Sure, if I can."

"Is there still a bartender working here that . . ." Herby gave him the description and what time it was when he was there.

"Oh, you mean Charles. Yeah, he still works here and on the same shift."

"Do you know if he works tomorrow night?" asked Herby.

"I think so. He's usually off Mondays and Tuesdays."

"Okay, thanks," Herby replied as he drank the rest of his 7-up, and then he said to Ed, "I gotta get home. My dinner is cold by now, and I don't like rocking the boat at home. I'm off

Saturday's and Sunday's, so you wanna meet here tomorrow night to talk to that bartender?"

"Alright. If you need me for anything, give ma a call, but you need not bother using the telephone," Ed quipped.

Herby laughed as they were starting to leave and said, "Okay, and I'll find out about that job too. I'm pretty sure they need a parts chaser."

Ed finished his 7-up and replied, "I'm gonna make a quick trip to Barstow to pick up some more of my shit."

As they were walking out of the door of Fergies, Herby said, "When?"

"Right now."

"See you tomorrow at Fergies then?"

CHAPTER EIGHT

Charlie

Twenty minutes later Ed was back on the freeway to Barstow. He'd learned his lesson about taking his driving so much for granted. The radio wasn't blaring this time, and he kept his speed down to the limit.

When Ed was cruising over Mountain Pass, he noticed a cloud of dust ahead of him on his right. As he drew closer, he realized what his car must have looked like when he rolled his on that very highway.

He pulled onto the shoulder and jumped out of his car. At that point he noticed that the wheels were still spinning on the up-side down car.

Ed walked up to the first car that slowed down to see what was going on and said excitedly, "Go to the nearest phone and call an ambulance!"

When the driver agreed and sped off, Ed ran as fast as he could toward the up-side down car, and when he approached it, he heard a voice in his head, but not a familiar one. When the desperate voice said, *"Help me! help me!"* Ed wondered if this silent call for help was coming from another anthropomorphic. *"Damn!"* Ed thought, *"I wonder how many of us there are?"*

"What?" the voice replied silently.

Ed peered into the car and saw a young man around his age laying on the roof holding his side, which was probably the reason he wasn't calling for help aloud. If the man had broken ribs, there was nothing Ed could do. Moving him could puncture a lung or something. Plus the man was obviously in agony.

Frustrating as it was, all Ed could do was wait for the ambulance. Unfortunately, it had to come all the way from Barstow, which was about 50 miles away.

Once the ambulance arrived and tended to the accident victim, they headed back to Barstow en-route to the same hospital where Ed was taken to previously. Ironically, the circumstances were very similar to his experience.

Ed followed the ambulance to the hospital to confirm his suspicion that the driver was, indeed, another anthro. He wondered if this was really coincidence or some kind of organized plan. *"If he is an anthro,"* Ed thought when he was pulling off the freeway, *"..like Herby, he might not be aware of his abilities."*

When Ed arrived at the hospital, he waited until he could talk to the attending physician, and meanwhile learned that Charlie Shoemaker had broken three ribs. He also suffered other cuts, scratches and contusions; furthermore, he had a concussion. Once Ed was satisfied that Charlie was going to be okay, he went home.

By the time he arrived at his mom's house, it was midnight, so he quietly entered his part of the house and went to bed.

Mrs. Smith awoke the next morning and got ready for work. She didn't realize that Ed was home until she walked outside to go to work and saw his car, so she assumed that he never left for Vegas in the first place, assuming that he probably got sidetracked by his friends or something. So she went on to work.

Ed intended on leaving for Vegas around six in the morning, but he overslept. Still in bed, he thought about the previous day's events. Since Ed was familiar with hospital routine, he figured this would be a good time to make contact: *"Charlie?"* Ed asked gently, *"Don't be alarmed if you can keep from it. Just hear me out. You're not dreaming. What's happening right now is really happening."*

"So I'm not dreaming?"

106

"No, you're not dreaming. Are you comfortable enough with this conversation to continue or should I wait?"

"I can hear you but it's gonna take some getting used to."

"That won't take long, Charlie. First of all, my name is Ed Smith, and I'm the one that found you right after your accident."

Charlie was laying there listening to Ed and responding, but not altogether sure that his cognitive functions was reliable.

"Before you start asking me questions, are you sure you're comfortable enough with this to continue right now?"

"Yeah," Charlie replied silently, *"I think so."*

"Can you stay awake for another hour or so?"

"Yes."

"Good, then I'll be there in about twenty minutes to talk to you in person, okay?"

"Aren't we talking now?" Charlie asked, not knowing what else to say or think.

"Yeah we are, but I think meeting in person will possibly make it more real. Don't you agree?"

"Uh . . . yeah, I suppose you're right, because this still feels like a dream, so yeah—c'mon over," Charlie said as he laid there wondering what the hell was going on. Was he just delirious from the concussion? Was he losing his mind? Or was it like the voice in his head said?

About twenty minutes later, Ed walked into Charlie's room, smiled, and said out loud, "Hi Charlie, I'm Ed Smith."

After shaking hands, Charlie looked at Ed suspiciously and said, "Hi."

"I'm here to convince you that you don't belong in the funny farm."

"I have to admit," Charlie replied in his head, *"I was beginning to wonder about that."*

107

Ed then smiled and said silently, *"I can't stay very long. I just wanted us to meet face to face to tell you that you're not crazy and that you're one of many people in the world who are referred to as anthropomorphics. Furthermore, you'll learn that, besides having the telepathic abilities we're experiencing right now, you also have other abilities that normal people don't have."*

"Other abilities?" Charlie asked..

"Yeah, but don't concern yourself with that. First let's get you comfortable with these silent conversations."

"I wanna know about the other abilities," Charlie said getting a little agitated.

"Shit! I shouldn't have mentioned that. Look, I really have to go. I probably should've waited to come here when I had more time. You see, I'm not all that familiar with all this either. I'm learning as I go, so please, don't rush me. I'm liable to do more harm than good, and I'm afraid I've already made mistakes telling you too much too soon, so before you start getting pissed off at me, give me a fucking break. The only reason I'm here right now is to help, but right now I have to go, so I'll be in touch," and then Ed turned around and walked out.

Ed returned home to pack up the rest of his things. As he was doing that he calmed down and thought he should make contact and apologize: *"Hey Charlie,"* Ed asked quietly.

"Yeah what?" he answered curtly.

"Hey, I'm sorry I got irritated, Charlie, but I'm under a lot of pressure right now and I probably didn't handle this right."

"I understand."

"Good. Right now I want you to relax and concentrate on getting better. All this will come together as we go."

"I hope so."

* * * *

During his lunch hour, Herby called Terry and told him that Ed wouldn't be back right away from Barstow. When he finished his lunch, he felt nauseous, so he laid down on the couch to see if his stomach would settle. Twenty minutes later he didn't feel any better, so he called in and took the rest of the day off. It was about nine 'clock when he finally awoke feeling better. When he got up, he needed to get out of there, so he said to his wife, "I'm going to the store for some beer."

"Okay, honey," Martha replied as though she were a loving wife, but really, she was putting on a facade for the sake of the kids. "Would you pick up a couple packs of cigarettes too, please?"

Walking out of the door, he replied, "Yeah, okay."

When Herby was unlocking his car, he knew right away what was happening to him as he lost consciousness. Like Ed being in a semi-conscious state while in a coma, now he was strangely aware, realizing that his recently acquired knowledge of his abilities as an anthro was responsible for making this possible.

He felt himself being carried and then placed into the back of a pick-up, the same pick-up and camper that Ed described. He then started a silent conversation: *"Hey Ed?"*

"Yeah."

"At this very moment I am unconscious and in the custody of kidnappers."

"Is that right?" Ed asked excitedly.

"Yeah," replied Herby, *"and it was nice of them to wait until you got out of the hospital, huh?"*

"I'll say," Ed replied as he arose from the couch at his mother's house, *"well, just go along with it and keep me posted."*

"I will," said Herby, and then he asked, *"by the way, why are you still in Barstow?"*

"I'd forgotten that this is the forth of July weekend, so I'm

109

staying here to watch the fireworks with my mom."

"That's good. I wish my mom was still alive," said Herby while he squirmed around to get comfortable, *"anyway, I called Terry and told him that you'd be awhile yet."*

"I'm glad you thought of that, because I forgot to get phone numbers from you before I left," Ed replied while he was walking into his bedroom, *"Oh!"* he added excitedly, *"something happened to me, too."*

Ed explained everything that happened concerning Charlie on his way to Barstow, and then he got all the phone numbers he needed.

After around fifteen minutes of city driving, Herby's kidnappers pulled off the main thoroughfare, and then felt the pick-up pull into a driveway and stop. As soon as the driver got out, Herby heard him say, "How's it going, Jerry?"

The old mobster replied, "Can't complain, kid."

Then Herby felt and heard the door of the camper shell open and the tailgate of the truck lowered.

One of the kidnappers had ridden in the back with Herby, obviously in case Herby were to wake up en-route to their destination. The driver grabbed his feet, and pulled him out as far as the tailgate, then the other fellow hopped out and took him by the shoulders. Herby could tell that he was being transferred to Jerry's vehicle.

Ed's suspicions about Trip's dad were now confirmed. After telling Trip about waking up at Friendly Fergie's, he hadn't told her anything more. He didn't want her to know what he suspected about her father.

Once Herby was placed in the back seat of Jerry's car, he could only hear the sound of voices, not what they were saying until Jerry opened his car door to get in.

"Okay guys, be talkin' to ya, eh."

110

Jerry started his car, and while en-route to some other location, Herby summoned his fellow anthro, *"Hey Ed?"*

"Yeah man, I've been on pins and needles waiting for you. What's happenin?"

"These are probably the same guys that got me before, but I'm sure I'm in the same truck and camper that you told me about. Another thing too, Ed: guess whose car I'm in the back seat of right now?"

"I bet it belongs to Jerry Galloway."

"Yep."

"So what's happenin now?"

"Nothin yet, but I'll get back to you."

After entering a driveway, the vehicle stopped. Jerry got out and opened the back door. As Herby was being carried into a building, he sneaked a peek at the name plate on the door: Dr. Dennis Selph, Psychiatrist.

Once they'd gotten Herby inside, Jerry said, "I'll be in the waiting room, doc, when you're ready," and he walked down the corridor leaving Herby and the doctor alone in an examination room.

After the examination room door was closed, Herby patiently played along until the doctor was well into the hypnotizing process.

"Herby, the next voice you hear will be Jerry's, and that's the voice that you'll obey from that point on. Is that understood?"

Herby couldn't suppress his anger any longer. He stood up and spoke quite belligerently, right in the doctor's face: "No! It isn't understood Dr. Dennis Selph, and from this point on you will *obey* everything my voice says. Is *that* understood?"

The doctor appeared shocked, and then replied, "How can this be?"

111

"Never mind that, just answer my fucking question you old quack."

"Yes sir," the doctor replied sheepishly.

As they stood toe to toe, Herby said, "Sit down old man. I should beat the fuck out of you right now, but that would only alert that other scumbag in there, Mr. Jerry Galloway. Now then, I'm only going to explain this once motherfucker," Herby said as he poked his finger in the doctor's chest, "When you go back in there to get Jerry, he better not be the least bit suspicious, because if he is, he isn't gonna be a bit happy with you, and neither will I. From what I hear, Mr. Galloway is a thoroughly dangerous man. So, bring the fucking creep back in here and continue as though everything was going as planned."

The doctor obediently opened the examination room door, walked down the corridor, and called for Jerry. When Jerry entered the room, he displayed an affable smile and said, "Hi Herby, remember me, I'm Jerry."

"Hi Jerry," Herby calmly replied. Since he wasn't familiar with hypnosis and how people responded, he played it off the best he could.

"Herby, I need your help for a couple days."

Unsure of how best to respond, Herby kept quiet and avoided making eye contact by looking around the room.

Not getting the expected response, Jerry continued, "Let me explain. I'm aware that you and your wife aren't getting along so well, so it shouldn't be that hard for you to get away for a couple days. So, I'd be willing to pay you two thousand dollars right now, if you'll do something for me. Now Herby, if at any time you're uncomfortable with what's going on, just say so and we'll forget the whole thing, and you can keep the money anyway." Jerry then took a wad of bills out of his pocket and asked, "Well Herby, what do you say?"

Looking at the wad of money, he replied, "Yes."

"Good, good!" Jerry said excitedly, and then he counted out two thousand dollars, gave it to him and said, "I'll be back shortly kid."

While Jerry was gone, he said silently, *"Hey Ed?"*

"Yeah, what's happenin?"

"I don't have much time, but I need you here as soon as possible. It's important, so how long will it take for you to get here?"

"I was expecting something like this, so I've already got my bags packed. What's going on?"

"I've been paid two thousand dollars in cash to be gone for two days. I don't know where I'll be going, or what I'll be doing, so if you can get here soon enough, I wanna give you the money. I'll play it off like I'm giving it to my wife. You might need it for expenses. I have to go now, so get here as soon as you can, and I'll keep you posted."

"Alright, I'm on my way."

When the doctor entered the room, Herby pointed to a chair and said, "Sit down you old fucker." Herby wasn't by nature mean or violent, but he needed to appear that way or the doctor might not take him seriously. "You'll be a lot better off doing what I say, old man, because if you don't, I'm afraid you and Jerry wouldn't look very good laying here in pools of blood. Now listen: when I leave here with Jerry, wait until my friend comes to talk to you. He'll be here in a couple hours. If you don't wait, you'll make me angry, and you wouldn't like me when I'm angry. You got all this, old man?"

"Yes, I'll wait for your friend," the doctor replied submissively.

"Okay then, go get that fucking creep in there and do or say whatever you usually do or say."

The doctor meekly arose to comply with Herby's command. Herby grabbed him by the arm, looked right into his eyes, and said with hostile emphasis, "If you make him suspicious, doc, your fucking ass is mine. Under-fucking-stand?"

The doctor nodded his head and departed from the room with his tail between his legs.

Herby was sure that he played his part convincingly, so he waited for Jerry to return from the waiting room to see if he was right.

Herby was lying in the same position as he was when Jerry left the room.

"Are you ready to go, Herby?"

"Yes."

Jerry led the way and Herby followed. Once they were in the car, Herby asked, "Can we stop by my house so I can leave this money with my wife?"

"Not taking any chances of losing it, eh kid?" Jerry asked with a suspicious grin on his face.

Looking straight ahead, Herby replied, "Yes."

"Can't says I blame you, kid. Where do you live?"

"1564 Vegas Valley Drive."

* * * *

Before Ed left Barstow, he left a note for his mother:

Dear Mom,

I had to get back to Las Vegas. I stayed here too long as it is. I'll call you later, and give you my new address and telephone number. I love you.

Eddy

"*Hey Ed,*" Herby said silently as Ed was driving past Lake

114

Delores.

"*Yeah, I'm on my way now.*"

"*Good. I realize that Jerry can't hear our conversations, but I still prefer keeping them short.*"

"*Of course.*"

"*Okay, go to my house and pick up the money I told you about. Right now Jerry is taking me there so I can, supposedly, give it to my wife; however, I'm really gonna hide it outside for you. When you get there, tell him to park in front of my house. Then go under the car port. You'll see a dark blue 65 Mercury. The money will be next to the inside sidewall* of the right front tire.*"

To keep himself occupied on the way to Vegas, Ed silently said, "*Hey Charlie?*"

"*Yeah! Bout fucking time!*"

"*I've been really busy, damn it?*" Ed replied, starting to get a little annoyed, "*and you're not going anywhere.*"

"*Well, I'd like to practice communicating, you know? I've been trying to contact you, but I don't know how.*"

"*Look, we're gonna have to take this slowly. I'll show you how to contact me later, but not now, so be patient.*"

"*What the fuck am I supposed to do, Ed? I'm stuck in this fuckin hospital, unable to move without pain, and in the midst of it all, I suddenly have this thing with you going on that I don't think I want any part of.*"

After a noticeable silence, Ed realized that being preoccupied with what Herby was going through was causing anxiety that he shouldn't be taking out on this neophyte, "*Charlie . . . hey Charlie? . . . hey, I'm sorry man!*"

Charlie wouldn't answer.

"*Damn!*" Ed said to himself, "*what the fuck is wrong with*

115

me?" Ed was distressed now, so he turned to his ole ace in the hole.

"*Hey Bobby?*"

"*Yeah.*"

"*I'm not doing so good with Charlie?*"

"*All you can do is the best you can,*" replied Bobby reassuringly."

When Ed was approaching state line, he heard Herby calling him, but first he responded to Bobby: "*Hey, I gotta go, Herby's calling. I'll get in touch later, okay?*"

"*Okay.*"

"*Hey Ed?*" summoned Herby.

"*Yeah,*" Ed replied as he was pulling off the freeway to use the rest room.

"*I'm at McCarren Airport,*" said Herby, "*waiting to board a plane to Chicago, so you'll have to use some of that expense money, but first I need you to do something else.*"

"*No problem, what?*"

Herby then explained what occurred between him and the psychiatrist and then continued, "*so . . . you're gonna have to put on a convincing tough-guy act.*"

"*Alright, sounds like fun,*" replied Ed

"*Yeah kinda—movie stars do it all the time, so play it off the best you can,*" Herby explained, "*and get as much information as you can out of that doctor. He's waiting for you now.*"

"*Okay, see you in Chicago.*"

After getting the money, Ed went to Terry's. When he pulled up, Terry was getting ready to get in his car and leave. Just before he opened his car door, he said, "I was beginning to wonder if you were ever going to show up."

"Yeah, I finally made it, but I gotta leave again. I just stopped by to leave more of my stuff here."

Terry reached into his pocket, retrieved a key, and then handed it to Ed and said, "Here, I forgot to give this to you. I've been leaving the door unlocked ever since, just in case you showed up."

"You didn't have to do that."

"No harm done, this is a pretty good neighborhood, but now we can keep it locked again. No sense in tempting fate."

* * * *

"Hello."

"Say there, Big Head," Jerry said into a pay phone at McCarren Airport, "I'm getting ready to board a flight to Chicago right now, and I've got the kid with me." Jerry then told Big Head what time he and Herby would be there.

"Great, I'll be there to pick you up."

* * * *

Ed knocked on the back door of Dr. Selph's office. As the door started to open, Ed pushed it and knocked the shrink to the floor.

Ed looked at the doctor momentarily, and when he was convinced he wasn't hurt, he offered his hand to help him up and with feigned concern said, "Sorry about that old man, but I don't have much time and I need some information quick."

"Tell me what you want to know young man, and let's be done with it."

"Alright, why has my friend been kidnapped and brought here to be hypnotized?"

"I don't know."

"C'mon, you old fucker, don't make me angry—you wouldn't

117

like me when I'm angry. Now do you expect me to believe that you don't know? I mean, an organized crime figure has a man kidnapped on several occasions to have him hypnotized, and the hypnotist doesn't even know why he's doing the hypnotizing? Doc . . . I was born at night, but not last night."

"Let me explain, son. When your friend was brought to me, I was told in no uncertain terms that my job was to put him under hypnosis, and that's it. The rest, between Mr. Galloway and your friend, was to be executed without me or anyone else in the room."

For some reason, Ed believed what the doctor was saying, but in order to get more information out of him, he had to play it off a little longer.

"Furthermore," the doctor continued, "I insisted that nobody witness my method of hypnosis; therefore, we understood each other. So I hypnotized your friend without Mr. Galloway being present, and he interrogated him without me being present."

"*Hmmm . . . that makes sense,*" Ed said to himself while he held eye contact with the doctor momentarily, and then continued, "But if you wanted to find out what Mr. Galloway wanted with Herby, as a result of your hypnotism, don't stand there and fuckin tell me that you didn't find out."

Dr. Selph turned around and asked Ed to follow him into his office. When the doctor started to sit down at his desk, Ed said, "Hold it right there, you old quack." When the doctor hesitated, Ed went around and took the doctor's chair, sat down and said, "I'm the one in control here, so get away from that desk."

"You don't even have a gun, young man."

That's when Ed decided to take a change of strategy: "Do I need one, sir?" Ed replied amiably.

The doctor replied, "I think not." They held eye contact again momentarily, then the doctor continued, "I really don't know very much son, but I hope you never reveal the source of what

I'm about to say."

"I won't. There's nothing to be gained by snitching you off."

"Okay, there's an ex colleague of mine that lives in Chicago that's involved in organized crime. He gave me a call and told me that a man by the name of Jerry Galloway would be contacting me." Once the doctor was about finished, he summed up by saying, "Now, if I were to call Chicago and start asking question, it could prove to be very dangerous to my health and everybody concerned, including your friend."

"That won't be necessary, doc, Mr. Galloway and Herby are on their way to Chicago right now."

CHAPTER NINE

A New Ability

If Americans knew what really goes on in our national government, they'd be appalled. That's part of the reason why there's such a thing as 'top secret'.

At this point in 1969, and for several years previous, there were plans, strategies, and innovations being implemented for a nuclear war. In comparison to a nuclear war, Viet Nam really was merely a spat.

If there is a monetary gain possible in anything the government is involved in, then organized crime is also interested. On the other hand, the government tries to stay on top of all the activity that organized crime gets involved with.

Organized crime has spies and affiliations in all levels of government; of course our government also has spies and affiliations that have infiltrated organized crime.

Organized crime became aware of anthropomorphic phenomenon, and by doing so, the government also gained knowledge of it; therefore, the government also became aware of organized crime's involvement with Herby. The government realized that organized crime was only interested in anthros if they could manipulate them to serve them monetarily.

Ed Raley and John Campbell were FBI agents dispatched to O'Hare Airport from their Chicago office to make an arrest on one Jerry Galloway. Since the CIA didn't have an office in Chicago, the FBI was also directed to detain Mr. Galloway's traveling partner, James Herbert Matthews, until a CIA agent arrived. Mr. Matthews was thought to be under the influence of hypnosis. The FBI were interested in Jerry and the CIA were interested in Herby.

When Jerry and Herby disembarked, the FBI agents approached Jerry and agent Campbell asked, "Sir, are you Jerry Galloway?"

"Yes I am."

Herby was amused, thinking that this was turning into quite an adventure. At this inopportune time, Ed silently summoned him: *"Hey Herby?"*

"Not now!"

"Okay, later."

After identifying themselves, agent Campbell said, "Mr. Galloway, you're under arrest for investigation of kidnapping. You have the right to remain silent . . ."

Agent Raley then asked Herby, "Are you okay, sir?"

"Yes, I'm fine," Herby replied amicably, "And how are you today?"

Agent Raley noticed a subtle smirk on Herby's face, and then replied with a look of bewilderment, "Uh, I'm fine, sir, just fine." Agent Raley attributed Herby's behavior to being under the influence of hypnotic suggestion.

While Jerry was being handcuffed and taken into custody, Herby was detained until the C.I.A arrived.

* * * *

When Ed left Dr. Selph's office satisfied that the doctor told him everything he knew, he pulled into the nearest service station for directions to McCarren Airport. On the way, Ed wanted to find out if Charlie was still angry with him: *"Hey Charlie,"* Ed summoned silently as he turned down the radio.

"Yeah."

"Are you still pissed off at me?"

122

"No, I just hate it here. I can't even move without pain. I don't have anything to read, don't know anyone in this fuckin town, and I have conversations with someone without talking."

"Charlie, it isn't like I don't know what you're going through; you see, I was in that same hospital about four months ago from a car accident that I too had on the freeway to Las Vegas. I spent three months in the county hospital in San Bernardino. I was discharged about a month ago, so believe me, I can identify with what you're sayin."

Ed didn't mention that he was in a coma the whole time. By telling the quarter lie inside the half truth, it might've given Charlie some incentive to hang tough.

"Hmm . . .," pondered Charlie, *"that's quite a coincidence, especially both of us being, uh, what do you call us? uh, anfro,"*

"Anthropomorphics," Ed answered for him.

"Yeah, that."

When approaching the airport, Ed said: *"Charlie, I hate to cut you off again, buddy, but right now I'm in the middle of something important. I'll get back with ya, okay?"*

Ed bought a ticket for Chicago and was spending the time before his flight playing slot machines when he heard Herby:

"Hey Ed"

"Yeah."

"I couldn't talk awhile ago, because at that moment Jerry was being arrested by the FBI for kidnapping."

"Is that right?" Ed asked with zeal, *"I wonder how they found out?"*

"I don't know, but I'm convinced they didn't find out from the doctor."

"I agree," replied Ed, *"but I bet Jerry wouldn't."*

"Hell no, he wouldn't," then Herby asked, *"Hey, where are*

123

you now?"

"I'm at McCarren Airport," Ed replied as he pulled the handle on a one armed bandit, *"killing time until my flight leaves. And you?"*

"I'm at O'Hare Airport in a little interrogation room waiting for a CIA agent to pick me up."

"CIA?"

"Yeah, this is becoming quite an adventure," replied Herby as he sat there quietly.

"Wow! CIA, FBI, I should start calling you 007."

While this silent conversation was going on, the two FBI agents who arrested Jerry were outside the door of the interrogation room talking, and then he heard agent Raley say, "Here comes the CIA agent now."

When agent Griego got close enough to be recognized, he offered his hand and said, "Long time no see."

"Yes it has," replied agent Raley."

After shaking hands, agent Campbell asked, "So, which do you like the best, the FBI or the CIA?"

"I really can't say, except that I don't like either one of them."

"That's too bad. Anyway, your kidnap victim is sitting right inside this door," informed agent Campbell.

"Okay, I better get him over to the office. There's some VIPs waiting to see him," replied agent Griego.

The FBI agents took Jerry to the Cook County Jail and booked him, and agent Griego took Herby to the federal building.

The government in Washington D.C. intended to observe Herby in an attempt to learn what was at the heart of this enigma, but unfortunately for them, as well as for organized crime, none of them learned anything. Even Jerry was released with no charges filed.

* * * *

On his flight to Chicago, sitting next to a snoring passenger, Ed silently said: *"Hey Charlie."*

"What."

"Once I get to a telephone, I'll call my mom and have her bring you something to read."

"I suppose that'll help, but could you get her to bring me some heroin? They're not giving me enough pain killers."

"Yeah, right. Actually, you won't be there much longer, and they'll give you a scrip for pain when you're discharged."

"I hope it's morphine."

"Probably Percodan or Codeine.

* * * *

As Herby was sitting in the small office being bored, he thought about how convenient it would be to just get up and simply walk out of there. He also thought about what Ed had said about anthros having unnatural abilities. Then, agent Griego entered the room and sat down, but before he could speak Herby locked eyes with him causing the agent's facial expression to freeze – just as Herby's had done with Ed at the dam. Griego seemed stuck in a trance and after a minute or so of frozen silence Herby thought to himself. *"Hmm . . .I wonder if . . .?"* He got up and opened the door of the little room he was in, looking around a much bigger room with lots of people at desks. He turned to see that agent Griego was still frozen in the same position, staring mutely at where Herby had been sitting a moment ago, so Herby made eye contact with a woman sitting at one of the desks. *"Wow! I can't believe it!"* Then he made eye contact with someone at another desk, and it worked again. Frozen, trance-like silence. As he walked through the large room, he repeated it

125

with everyone in there. When he got to the other side of the room, he looked back and thought about what it would look like if all of those people resumed what they were doing. When he opened the last door to the building, he heard all the voices and typewriters working again. Walking down the street, he laughed out loud and thought, *"Wow! I can get used to this."*

Back in the office agent Griego suddenly looked around the room in search for Herby. Realizing that he was no longer there, he opened the door to the adjacent office and asked, "Have you seen Mr. Matthews?"

* * * *

Herby walked aimlessly for awhile on the side streets and alleyways until he found himself getting tired. All that he'd been through, plus jet lag, had taken it's toll, so he silently said, *"Hey Ed?"*

"Yeah, what's happenin now?"

"You won't believe it," and then Herby explained what took place at the federal building.

"Wow!" Ed exclaimed in awe, *"I wonder if we can leap buildings in single bound?"*

"Makes you wonder, huh?" After talking about it for awhile, Herby asked, *"Where are you right now?"*

"In the air, but it shouldn't be long before we land."

"Well, I don't know where in the fuck I am. I've never been in Chicago, so when you get off the plane, catch a cab and come to wherever I am."

"Okay."

When Ed disembarked, he made good his promise to Charlie by calling his mother and asking her to take some reading material to him at the hospital. He didn't bother explaining to

126

her where he was, so he just let her assume that he was calling from Las Vegas. In 1969 there was no such thing as caller ID.

When Herby got into a cab with Ed, they told the driver to take them somewhere near a bus station where there was a place to have breakfast and rent a motel room. They didn't figure it was a very good idea to go back around the airport. The cab pulled up to a motel, and the driver pointed to a cafe across the street, so Ed paid the driver, and they went to the cafe and ordered a meal. As they were waiting, Ed took out his wallet and gave Herby a wad of money and said out loud, "Here, I believe this is yours, what's left of it."

Herby took it and peeled fifty dollars off the top and said, "Take this, you need pocket money."

"Thanks," Ed replied as he put it in his pocket. "By the way, why didn't you stick around the federal building to see what happened?"

"If I knew that I could've left anytime I wanted, I probably would have, but I was getting claustrophobic. Plus, I didn't think they had the right to keep me there against my will, and I wasn't sure how someone under the influence of hypnosis was supposed to act."

"Yeah, I think you made the right choice; besides, they would've said that keeping you in custody was for your own good."

"No doubt."

"I wonder who they thought was under the influence of what, when you walked out of there like that?"

They were laughing light-heartedly when their meal was brought to them, then their conversation subsided, and they ate voraciously. Once they lit up their after-meal cigarettes, Ed said, "You know, between the government and organized crime, somewhere along the line, they're probably going to get you again."

"Yeah, and maybe then I'll go along for the ride to see what it is they're after."

"You don't know?"

"I think I do. I think organized crime wants to exploit this anthropomorphic phenomenon and try to manipulate it."

"Yeah, and then somehow the government got wind of it, and decided to bogart you for themselves."

"Better the government than organized crime, I suppose," Herby said while looking around the empty cafe.

The waitress walked up and asked if everything was alright, and Ed replied, "Yes, ma'am, and if you'll give us the check, we'll be on our way."

They left her a tip, paid the bill, and on the way out of the cafe, Ed asked, "I'd like to get involved with all this too, why should you get to have all the fun?"

"You can have it all for all I care. I have a family, and a job to get back to."

They got a room with two single beds, and both of them flopped down and were asleep within minutes.

When they got up Ed said, "Let's get cleaned up and get out of here. I don't trust the government anymore than I do organized crime."

As Herby was preparing to get into the shower, he said, "Maybe we should figure out a way to put them on to you instead of me."

"Good idea," replied Ed, but we should get you home first.

An hour later, they were on a bus to the next town because they didn't want anyone nosing around and finding bus tickets bought for Las Vegas by two men traveling together. When they got off the bus, they went to the ticket office and then bought tickets to Las Vegas. However, they had to wait for four hours.

128

"Now what?" Herby asked as they left the ticket office window.

"Let's find a bar and get drunk," Ed suggested.

"I thought you quit drinking?"

"No, I just stopped temporarily, but now I'm starting again, so let's find that bar."

It wasn't a very big town, so it didn't take long to find a saloon. They sat at the bar and ordered beer. There were only a few people there, and there wasn't any music playing on the juke box, so Herby went over to play some. By the time he returned to the bar, Credence Clearwater Revival's *Proud Mary*, was drowning out other conversations. "They sure talk funny around here," Ed said when Herby returned.

"I know, and sometimes it's hard to figure out what the hell they're sayin."

"Wanna play some pool?"

"Alright."

They started playing pool, and within a couple hours they had a buzz on. By that time they were playing partners against a couple other guys. Ed and Herby were better-than-average pool players, and as their buzz increased, they continued winning. Before long, they found themselves, not only teasing their opponents for losing, but they started mocking their eastern accents. The bartender, and a couple of the other patrons watched the pool games as tension mounted. Then the bartender made a statement to his customer's at the bar, "Those two strangers are cruisin for a bruisin."

"I think you're right," replied a rowdy patron at the bar, "and I'm going to help give it to em when the shit comes down."

Ed and Herby were drunk by this time, and before Ed knew it, his buddy was laid out on the floor, and there were a couple of angry looking guys coming at him. He remembered what Herby did at the government building, so he quickly made eye

129

contact with one of them, and sure enough, it stopped him in his tracks—this caused the other guy to bump into him. Ed walked around the pool table and made eye contact with the second guy. Then he froze the bartender. It wasn't long before everyone in the place looked like what the federal building employees looked like. About that time Herby stirred, "uh . . what hap . . ."

"Never mind that," Ed interrupted, 'right now let's get the fuck out of here."

When Herby got up, he looked around on the way out, laughed, and replied, "Oh, I see Superman's been here."

They returned to the bus station just in time to board the bus. Four days later on the 12th of July, a greyhound bus entered the Las Vegas bus terminal, and Herby and Ed were two of the passengers that got off. They hailed a cab and went to McCarren airport to pick up Ed's car. When they were leaving the airport Ed said, "Herby, I've decided to go back to Barstow. It's been fun, interesting, and sometimes a little dangerous, but since my dad died, my mom's been there alone. I need to be there. Of course I'll come to your rescue again if the wolves get to you again."

"I understand," replied Herby. After a couple minutes of silence, he added, "You know what? I'm gonna tell Trip, my girlfriend, about you. She'll probably tell her dad about it, then maybe they'll start picking on you for awhile. Old Jerry won't be able to pass that up, you know." Herby said.

"Hell no, he won't. I'll try to make it up here again in two weeks, so you might as well start feeding her information this weekend. That way you'll have time to figure out how best to approach her."

"Yeah, I'll do that."

When they pulled up to the signal at Vegas Valley Drive and Maryland Parkway, Herby asked, "Would you pull into that 7-11 there. I'm gonna need some beer for this."

"Sure, but me, I'm quitting again. I don't want it any more." Ed replied as he parked in front of the store.

When Ed dropped Herby off at home, they said their goodbyes, and Ed went to Terry's to pick up his stuff. It was five o'clock in the afternoon. Terry wasn't home from work yet, so once Ed was all packed up and ready to leave, he left a note:

Terry,

> *I've decided not to live in Las Vegas after all. I appreciate your offer and generous hospitality. The next time I'm in Vegas, Herby and I will come over and see you.*

Your new friend, Ed

* * * *

When Jerry was released from the Cook County Jail without charges filed, his crime partner, Big Head, was there to pick him up.

"Did you have a nice rest?" Big Head asked in jest.

"I did, but it wasn't exactly a vacation paradise, you know."

"What else would you call it? Three hots and a cot, plus free medical coverage. That's better than you pay your help."

"Uh huh. Anyway Big Head, did you put anyone on that fuckin old quack in Vegas?"

"I didn't, but Dr. Dennis Selph is no longer in practice, and he's nowhere to be found."

"Uncle Sam probably has him in the witness protection program with a brand new identity, huh?"

"I'm afraid so," replied Big Head, "which convinces me that

131

he's the one that tipped off the feds."

Jerry spent a couple of days with Big Head, and then caught a flight back to Las Vegas and back to the drawing board.

Herby's mysterious disappearance foiled the CIA's investigation and interfered with the efforts of organized crime.

Ed was again back at home in Barstow. When Mrs. Smith arose on her day off the following morning and entered the living room, she peered out of her front window and saw her son's car. She assumed he was just back to pick up more of his things.

About noon on this hot summer day, he entered the living room and said, "Hi mom."

"Good morning, baby. Back to get some more of your things?"

"No, I'm moving back in, Mom. I changed my mind about Vegas."

When she looked at Ed, he could tell she was pleased, "I'm glad, honey, it's been awfully lonely around here without you."

"I won't be living here forever, mom."

"I know, but you're here now," she said. Ed gave his mother a hug and then asked, "Can I fix you some breakfast?"

"Thought you'd never ask."

After Ed finished breakfast, he talked with his mother for awhile before he showered and got dressed to go to the hospital to see Charlie. When Ed entered the room, he saw that Charlie was out of his bed and gazing out of a window. "You don't look like you're in such bad shape to me." Ed said aloud as he entered the room.

Charlie turned around and said, "Let me break three of your ribs and let's see how you feel."

"Wa, wa, wa. You look fine to me," jested Ed with a smile.

132

"By the way," inquired Charlie, "what about this horrible three months that you spent in here? That must have been awful."

For the time being, Ed didn't admit to the coma: "Oh yeah, it was terrible, Charlie—day in and day out I . . ."

Charlie listened momentarily in mock belief, and then interrupted, "Save it, Ed. Don't piss on my back and try to tell me I'm sweating. I know about your coma."

"Oh," Ed replied sheepishly.

"Anyway, I'm getting out of here tomorrow."

"Hey, that's great. I bet you're glad."

The following morning, a silent voice woke him up: *"Hey Ed."*

Ed awoke, rubbed the sleep out of his eyes, and replied, *"Hey Charlie, what's up?"*

"It's noon, man, you said you'd be here at ten to pick me up."

"Oh yeah . . ." Ed replied groggily as he yawned and stretched, *"I'm sorry Charlie, I overslept. I'll be there in about twenty minutes, okay?"*

"Alright, I'll be in the waiting room."

Twenty minutes later Ed walked into the waiting room, and within minutes, a nurse was pushing Charlie out to Ed's car in a wheelchair.

In jest Ed said, "If you think I'm gonna push you around in that thing all day, you're nuts."

Just as the nurse stopped short of the car, Charlie looked up at Ed and replied, "You have to Ed, and you have to load me up and unload me every . . ."

The nurse cut Charlie short by saying, "Don't listen to him, this is hospital policy, all patients leaving the property is in a wheelchair."

Charlie snarled exaggeratingly at the nurse, got out of the wheelchair, and said, "I had him going and you blew it."

The nurse turned the wheelchair around and said cheerfully, "Good riddance, Charlie, and please take care of yourself."

As she departed, Charlie replied, "Okay, Debbie, thanks for everything."

A month later Charlie was still living with Ed and his mother. Mrs. Smith grew fond of him and vice versa. Furthermore, Charlie was a help to her around the house. In return he wasn't charged rent for staying there while he recuperated.

Ed orientated his new friend as much as he felt was necessary, and he also explained some of his and Herby's experiences

It was the middle of August when Ed and Charlie took the Tropicana off ramp into Vegas, where they found a phone booth.

Before Ed got out of the car, he pointed his finger and said, "See that sign over there that says Churchill Downs Sports Book?"

"Yeah."

"That's Jerry Galloway's operation."

"Oh yeah?" Charlie replied when they were getting out of the car.

"Todkill Lincoln-Mercury," said the voice on the other side of Ed's phone line.

"Parts department, please," Ed replied.

"Will you please hold?" Without waiting for an answer, she placed Ed on hold.

A couple minutes later, Herby answered: "Parts department."

"Hey, what's goin on?"

"I knew when you said," replied Herby with a wisp of scorn

in his voice, "that you wouldn't be back in Vegas in two weeks."

"I couldn't help it," replied Ed without explaining why.

"Where are you, anyway?"

"Out on the strip, but listen: remember the anthro I told you about that I found on the freeway?"

"Yeah."

"Well, I brought him with me, so we'll be by there to pick you up when you get off."

When Herby got off work, he got into the back seat of Ed's car. "Herby, this is Charlie Shoemaker. Charlie, this is Jim Matthews, but we call him Herby."

The two men shook hands and exchanged greetings and a little small talk, while Ed was busy trying to start his car.

"Is this old thing going to start?" Herby asked.

"It's never done this before," replied Ed, still grinding on the starter.

"Don't run the battery down," Herby said as he was getting out of the car.

"Why don't we start it telepathically," Charlie said jokingly.

As soon as Charlie said that, he could tell by the looks his new friends gave him, that he shouldn't have said that.

"Okay, try to start it now, Ed," Herby said as he placed his hand over the top of the carburetor. The motor turned over a couple of times and then started, barely, because the battery was low. When Herby got back in the car, he said, "Where do ya wanna go?"

"How about Friendly Fergie's for old times sake?" Ed asked in a manner that suggested to Charlie that his slip of the tongue was forgiven.

"Yeah okay, let's go," Herby replied amicably, as he turned around and looked at Charlie, "That's the place I woke up after I was hypnotized the first time."

"Is that right?" was Charlie's tremulous response.

When they pulled up to Fergie's, Ed turned off the motor and asked, "Is this old thing gonna start again?"

"Yeah," Herby replied while getting out of the car, "the battery is charged now. Somebody changed the generator that was originally in this old car to an alternator, otherwise we would've needed a battery charge.

Herby ordered a pitcher of beer. When Ed ordered a 7-up, he excused himself to make a phone call.

"Hello."

"Hey, Terry."

"Yeah Ed, what's happenin?"

"Oh, not much. Me and a friend of mine are here for a short visit. What have you been up to?"

"Not much, really, I just got off work, and was just getting ready to jump in the shower. Where are you, anyway."

"Friendly Fergie's. We just picked up Herby from work, and decided to come over here for a drink."

"Why don't you guys come over here, I've got plenty to drink."

"I don't drink anymore, Terry, but these guys do, so we'll be over after they finish this pitcher of beer."

"Okay, see you in awhile then," Terry said.

When Ed returned to the bar, Charlie and Herby weren't there, so he went looking around in the slot machine area and found them.

"Let's go!" Ed yelled over the noise of the slots.

"Go where? Herby asked as he pulled a slot machine handle, "We just got here."

"I know, but the drinks here cost money," Ed yelled in reply. "I just called Terry, and he invited us out there to help him drink his beer."

"I should've thought of that," Herby replied, "He always has a lot of beer."

Terry lived in Henderson at the time, and when they arrived, he was waiting for them outside. When Ed, Charlie, and Herby approached Terry, Ed introduced Charlie, and then they all went inside.

The next morning around ten o'clock, Ed woke up in what was to be his room before he changed his mind about living there.

Meanwhile, Charlie was lying awake on the couch in the living room. He thought about his ability to communicate with these guys without uttering a word, then he recalled how sensitive Ed and Herby were about it when he made a joke.

Charlie didn't have Ed and Herby's experience with anthropomorphic abilities, so what he knew about it was what they told him about their experiences. He was feeling apprehensive and overwhelmed with it all, plus he wasn't supposed to make jokes about it or use his abilities unless it was absolutely necessary. He felt like a kid being told to stay out of the cookie jar. Because of all this, he felt compelled to escape their tyranny. He liked them alright, but he was torn between what he knew he should do and what he wanted to do. What he wanted to do won out, so with no further thought, Charlie quietly got up and left.

They didn't know Charlie left, and after laying in bed for another half hour or so, Ed got up to see why it was so quiet in the house. When he entered the living room, it was empty, so he looked in Terry's bedroom, only to find it empty, too. Being a weekday, he assumed that Terry went to work, but what about Charlie and Herby? "*Hey Herby*," Ed inquired silently.

"*Yeah*," answered Herby as he gave a customer his change.

137

"*Where's Terry and Charlie?*"

"*When Terry and I left for work, Charlie was still asleep on the couch.*"

"*Well, he ain't here now. Maybe he went for a walk or something.*"

"*Yeah, probably. Hey, another customer just came in, so I'll talk to you later.*"

CHAPTER TEN

Dealing with Charlie

When Ed got off the phone, he summoned his old friend, *"Hey Bobby."*

"Yeah."

"I need your opinion on something."

"Okay."

"Fist of all, did you know that there are more anthros in our respective existences?"

"I've often wondered about that," replied Bobby, *"if you think about it, it doesn't make sense that we're the only ones. I'm guessing you've run into one."*

"I have. I've found one who isn't aware of his abilities, and Herby and I agree that he'll probably use his abilities for selfish or entertainment purposes."

"As you know, I'm not an expert on all of this, but I think we're on the right track consulting each other when things come up. If I run into another anthro in my universe, I'm probably gonna need your help figuring out what to do, so in my opinion, I don't think you should invest much time and effort worrying about it. You guys have your own problems, and if you're right, he'll probably hang himself with his own rope."

"I was hoping you'd say something like that."

"All we can do is the best we can, right?"

"Right."

* * * *

While Charlie was walking along the Boulder Highway in Las Vegas, he'd turn around every minute or so and look for Ed's car. The old 48 Chevy Sedan that Ed was then driving would be easy enough to spot with its bright green color. He saw a bar ahead, and decided to go in and kill a couple hours, giving Ed time to give up looking for him, if that's what he was doing. Being in a bar drinking beer, he couldn't help thinking about what happened to Ed and Herby at that bar in Chicago. About half way through his beer, he wondered why Ed and Herby avoided conversations about anthros when they were around him. With his thoughts running like a squirrel in a squirrel cage, he wondered how many of these unnatural abilities he was capable of. He also thought about how insensitive Herby and Ed were about the pain his ribs had been giving him since they'd been together. He was thrilled with having the uncanny ability to communicate telepathically, but was uncomfortable communicating with other anthros who wanted to control him. He decided then and there that he'd show them a thing or two, so when he finished his beer, he held eye contact with the bartender momentarily, and then smugly walked out of the bar with a shit-eating grin on his face. Knowing that there was no harm done, since there wasn't anybody else in the bar, he released the man when he was about twenty yards away. Two hours later Charlie was standing on the Tropicana on-ramp with his thumb out. Three and a half hours after that, he was standing on an on-ramp in Barstow. He really didn't know where he was going—he was just going. An old Ford pick-up pulled over, and just as he was approaching the passenger door, he got blasted in the face with a water balloon. When the pick-up sped off leaving Charlie standing there soaking wet, the driver looked over his shoulder laughing. Charlie was able to make eye contact with him. As a result, the driver's foot was frozen on the accelerator, thereby causing the truck to jump a curb and roll down a steep embankment. After rolling a couple times the truck landed on it's wheels. After witnessing what he caused, he ran to the service station across the street from the on-ramp and said to the attendant excitedly, "Call the police and an ambulance! Bad accident!"

The attendant stopped what he was doing and complied. Meanwhile, Charlie started back toward the accident site, which had ended up on the median, but stopped where he was hitch hiking from. He saw no sense in returning to the scene, but while standing there, he remembered that he hadn't released the driver. After doing so, the driver got out of the pick-up and looked his truck over, obviously analyzing the extent of the damage. The driver wasn't hurt, but when the driver turned his attention to his buddy still in the truck, he was horrified. He then turned and looked up at Charlie standing on the on-ramp.

Charlie smiled and waved at him, but when the sirens started screaming, he casually walked away before he got involved as a witness. He started having reprehensible feelings about himself. *"No fuckin wonder Herby and Ed act the way they do toward me,"* Charlie thought while walking along main street. He decided to postpone his trip to nowhere. After thinking about it for awhile, he felt compelled to find out about the accident victim. That was the least he could do to assuage his guilty feelings since he was the one that caused the accident in the first place. He was somewhat familiar with the Barstow area from his stay in the hospital and when he stayed with Ed and his mother. When he arrived at the hospital, he went to the receptionist's window of the emergency room and asked, "I'd like to inquire about the two guys who were just brought in from the accident on the freeway?"

After being asked to wait a few minutes, she said, "The driver is fine, not a scratch, but the other man is in serious condition, but not on the critical list."

"Thank you ma'am," replied Charlie as they exchanged smiles.

141

Satisfied that he wasn't responsible for killing anyone, he left the hospital.

Ed decided to return to Barstow, but first he left Terry a note thanking him for his hospitality, and then went to where Herby worked to say goodbye to him. When he entered the parts department, Herby was busy with a customer. When the customer left, Herby asked, "Why don't you stick around till I get off for lunch? I'll buy."

"Alright, I'll wait for you in my car," Ed replied as he walked out. He listened to his car radio as it played, *The Eve of Destruction*, by Barry McGuire.

When Herby got into the car, he said, "That's a good song."

Ed started his car and replied, "Yeah, I think so too."

"Have you ever had a buffet lunch at a casino?" Herby asked.

"No, but I see them advertised all over the place, and on the radio."

During their meal, Ed said, "Since Charlie's gone, I guess we can't get your girlfriend's dad interested in him now."

"Maybe we can."

"But he won't answer when I summon him."

"Eventually, I think he will, and if or when he does, just apologize for both of us, then ask him to come back."

"I hope you're right. Okay, we'll wait, and if he does contact me, hopefully I'll be able to persuade him to come back, then you can start telling your girlfriend about him."

"Exactly, and then hopefully we can have him move in with Terry like you were going to do."

"Sounds like a plan."

After they gorged themselves on the, all-you-can-eat, buffet, Ed took Herby back to work, gassed up, and headed for Barstow.

142

When Herby arrived home from work, he found an envelope on the dining room table with "Herby" written on it. Before he opened it, he felt a pang in the pit of his stomach and chest:

Dear Herby,

I am sorry it has to be this way, but it's not working between us anymore. We've been secure, but not happy. I'm sure you, as I do, realize that this was inevitable. Writing this is hard for me, so I hope we can still be friends. I think that you'll agree that the kids should stay with me rather than with you and your girlfriend.
We'll talk later.

I do love you,

Martha

Rather than think himself into a depression, he called his girlfriend.

"Hello," answered Jerry.

Herby smiled when he heard that familiar voice, and then with a disguised voice, he asked, "Is Teri there?"

"Hold on, pal," Jerry replied sarcastically.

Herby then heard the old man say, "Telephone Teri."

She picked up the phone in her room, and then yelled, "I got it in here, daddy!" When she heard the click, she answered,

"Hello?"

"Hey, would your dad have called you to the phone if I'd asked for Trip?"

"Yeah, but he doesn't like it."

"Good thing I asked for Teri then."

"Yeah," Trip replied, and then changed the subject, "This is Thursday, isn't it?"

"It is. Aren't I allowed to call you on Thursdays?"

"Sure, but it's so unexpected, that's all."

"Never mind, I'll call back some other time?"

"What's the matter, Herby?"

After being silent momentarily, he replied, "Oh, nothing much, my wife left me is all."

"Oh Herby, I'm sorry. Uh, no I'm not . . ., yes I am . . ., I.."

"I know you are – and you aren't. I feel the same way," responded Herby empathetically.

"I'm glad you understand. Uh, you want to get together?"

"Yeah."

"How about we meet at the Foxfire Lounge on Nellis boulevard?" Trip asked with a comforting voice.

Herby sat at the bar waiting. It'd been quite awhile since he'd enjoyed her company, and now he was thankful for her companionship. He felt lucky that she waited for him as long as she had, because most respectable women aren't comfortable having affairs with married men. However, she knew that Herby loved her and was aware of his domestic problems at home. When she arrived, they greeted each other with a hug and a kiss. When the passion of the moment subsided, Trip said, "If you keep kissing me like that, I'm going to be really happy that your wife left."

When they sat down, Herby replied, "I'm pretty sure you're happy about that anyway."

"Yes, I suppose I am."

"I know that I love you."

Being caught off guard, she beamed and then replied, "Herby, you've never told me that before."

"I should have, because I think I've been taking you too much for granted. I don't deserve you, really."

"Herby, I hope this isn't just an emotional defense mechanism. Think about it honey, you've never said these things to me before."

The bartender approached and took their order. When he left, Herby replied, "I suppose that's one way of looking at it, but look at it this way: since I'm obviously not the type to verbalize my affections, maybe this trauma has provoked me to say things that I've felt all along."

Just as they were separating from another emotional embrace, the bartender said, "Two dollars, please."

Once they were comfortable in a booth, Trip asked, "Where ya been lately, anyway?"

"Well, it's a long story," Herby replied, explaining a story based on the truth, but modified to suit the circumstances. He explained Ed's indirect involvement as a consultant, but implicated Charlie as an arcane partner. He told her about finding Charlie on the freeway in an overturned car; furthermore, he substituted the Valley Hospital in Las Vegas for the Barstow Hospital. He cleverly kept her on the edge of her seat with the half truth inside of the quarter of a lie.

"You mean you have extra sensory perception?" Trip asked, displaying an obvious air of awe.

"I guess that's what it is," replied Herby feigning ignorance.

"Wow! that's amazing.

"Yeah."

"Hmm," Trip said hesitatingly, "If I didn't know you so well, I'd. . .."

Cutting her off, he replied, "I know, some crazy shit, huh?"

"I'll say. No wonder I haven't heard from you, and no wonder your wife left. She probably suspects you're having an affair or something, and I assume you haven't confided any of this to her?"

"Hell no, she'd think I went off the deep end."

"Do you still have your job?"

"Yes, I don't know for how long though. I have a good boss; we've been friends for a long time, and I've assured him that everything will be coming together for me soon."

As usual, they spent the night together in a motel. Between their intervals of making love, Herby let Trip know only as much as he wanted her dad to know.

Herby felt bad about having to use her this way, but it wasn't like he was really *using* her. He *was* in love with her, so he naturally hoped that things could be resolved without her affection for her dad being compromised.

On the way to Barstow, Ed tried to summon Charlie a couple of times, but he wouldn't respond. When he arrived home, his mother was in her bedroom asleep, so he went to his bedroom and turned on his record player. After dozing off, he awoke about an hour later when he heard the washing machine in the adjacent room. He decided to try again: "*Hey Charlie.*"

Charlie heard Ed alright, but didn't respond. He thought, "*I really should answer him, but he's the one that said that I was to only use this ability when absolutely necessary?*" Then he asked himself, "*What if he's in some kind of trouble?*" He decided that if, or when Ed called on him again, he'd respond.

An hour later, when Charlie was 30 miles from Barstow in

146

Victorville, he heard Ed's voice again: "*Hey Charlie.*"

"*Yeah,*" Charlie finally replied, reluctantly.

"*Bout time you answered me.*"

"*You guys pissed me off,*" Charlie replied in defense.

"*We're aware of that, man, but we knew of no other way to relate the importance of what we had no words for, you know? Hey, we're new at this, too, and we're doing the best we can, and are trying not to fuck things up.*"

"*Alright, I probably did act hastily, but this is heavy shit, man. I keep expecting to wake up,*" Charlie replied, starting to feel a little guilty for reacting so dramatically. Charlie then explained everything that happened to him in Barstow with the water balloon incident. "*So,*" he continued, "*I suppose it took something tragic like that to make me realize that these abilities really do need to be using sparingly.*"

"*Well, too bad somebody had to get hurt.*"

"*Yeah, I know.*"

"*Say,*" Ed said questioningly, "*would you consider returning to Vegas?*"

"*Uh . . . Why?*"

"*We need your help.*"

"*You know, after what I just went through, I'm tired as hell. If I started hitchhiking back there now I'd probably die of exhaustion. My ribs are still bothering me from all the runnin, and all that excitement back there, I . . ..*"

"*Where are you?*"

"*Victorville,*" Charlie replied hesitatingly.

"*But where at in Victorville?*

"*Uh, ..the Palmdale Road on-ramp to San Bernardino.*"

"*If you'll agree to help us, I'll pick you up in 45 minutes.*"

147

"*You must be at your mom's house.*"

"*Yeah, I am.*"

"*Alright, I'll be waiting for you in the Holiday Inn coffee shop.*"

When Ed walked in finding Charlie sitting at a booth looking haggard, he smiled and said, "*You look like death sitting on a corner eating life savers.*"

Charlie just looked at him and then sneezed.

Without taking a seat, Ed said, "*C'mon, let's go back to Barstow first, and let my mom nurse you back to health.*"

"*Okay.*" As they approached Ed's old car, Charlie noticed something that Ed obviously missed: "*Ed, before you get in, you should probably change that flat tire.*"

Standing there looking at it, Ed said, "Shit!" He changed the tire, and when he got in to start it, Charlie was already asleep in the back seat. Ed was tired too, so once they entered the house, they wasted no time going to bed, but before Ed went to sleep, he silently said, "*Hey Herby.*"

Herby and Trip were also about to go to sleep when Herby replied, "*Yeah.*"

"*I got him.*"

"*You mean Charlie?*"

"*Yeah.*"

"*How soon will you guys be back?*"

"*It'll be at least a week, because he's sick.*"

"*Sick?*"

"*Yeah, you should see him—he looks terrible and sounds worse, so me and my mom are going nurse him back to health first.*"

"*Okay. I'll start working on Trip in the morning.*"

* * * *

A week later on the first of September, 1970, Herby was working when he heard Ed's voice: *"Hey Herby."*

Before Herby had a chance to respond, he heard Charlie's voice: *"Hey Herby."*

"Hmm . . .," Herby thought, *"We've never tried a three-way conversation."* He concentrated on Ed first and responded: *"Hold on Ed, Charlie's also calling. Let's see if we can do a three-way conversation."* Herby then responded to Charlie: *"I'm in silent contact with Ed right now, so I want you to concentrate on him too to see if we can have a three-way conversation."* After concentrating on Charlie, Herby asked: *"How are you feeling, Charlie?"*

"Fine, now, the hospital couldn't have done better to nurse me back to health as Ed's mom."

"That's good," replied Herby.

The three-way conversation went well and a couple days later Ed and Charlie were on the freeway back to Vegas. *"So where ya want to meet in about an hour?"* asked Ed when they were passing Mountain Pass.

"I get off work soon, so how about Fergie's again?"

Once the conversation with Herby was over, Charlie asked Ed aloud, "What makes you think Jerry will try to get to me if he hasn't attempted it on Herby again."

"Hopefully, he'll think that you'll be easier to manipulate. You see, he didn't do very well with Herby; besides, pursuing Herby landed him in jail, but on the other hand, I doubt that he's ruled Herby out."

"I guess having two of us to use is better than one."

"I'm sure that's the way he's looking at it."

An hour later, they parked at Friendly Fergie's.

149

As Ed turned off the motor, he said, "Here we are again."

"Yep, here we are," Charlie replied as he opened his door, eager to get inside to have a beer.

"Lock it, Charlie," Ed said while pushing down the lock mechanism and closing the door.

When Herby turned around and saw his fellow anthros, he smiled and said jokingly, "Bout time, a man could get drunk waiting on you guys."

They all shook hands and then Herby asked, "Want a beer Charlie?"

"Yeah, I'll take a bud."

"And I know what you want, Ed."

"While we're waiting, I'll go call Terry," Ed said as he got off the bar stool.

Herby and Charlie exchanged small talk for awhile, and then Ed returned and said, "He wasn't home, but I called his work and they said he just left, so I'll call again in a few minutes."

"Did he ever get a roommate?" asked Charlie, directing his question to Herby.

"I don't know. I haven't seen or talked to him lately."

They arrived at Terry's house in Henderson about eight o'clock, and again Terry was outside awaiting their arrival. They greeted each other and entered the house, at which point Terry's guests smelled the sizzling barbecue coming from outside the back door.

"Hey, that smells good!" Charlie said when they got inside.

"You guys like pork chops?" asked Terry.

"Everybody likes pork chops," replied Ed.

"Another thing guys," added Terry, "I figure since I'm supplying the food and women, the least you guys could do is supply the booze."

150

"Women!" Ed and Charlie replied in unison.

"Yeah women; you know what they are, they usually have long hair with these growths on their chests, and . . .."

"Yeah yeah," replied Ed, "We'll be right back. Ya want anything besides beer?"

"Get whatever ya want," replied Terry as he walked out of the back door to tend the barbecue."

On the way to the store, Herby said, "I'll call Trip when we get to the store and ask her to join us. This is a good time for her to meet you, Charlie."

"How much have you told her about me?"

"I told her that you were in Chicago with me instead of Ed."

"So she don't know about Ed at all, huh?" asked Charlie.

"No."

Charlie went in the store and Herby went to a pay phone.

"Hello," answered Trip.

"Hi there," replied Herby.

"Hi honey!" Trip responded excitedly, "What'cha doing?"

"Oh, just wondering if you'd like to come to a barbecue?"

"I don't know, Herby. I don't know any of your friends."

"My new friend Charlie is there."

"You mean the one that you've been communicating with telepathically?" Trip asked, obviously interested.

"Yeah, but don't let em know that you know, okay?"

"I won't," she replied hesitatingly, "Ya know, I'm not comfortable being around people who know I'm your concubine?"

"Don't sweat it, they're not gonna judge you; besides there'll be other women there."

151

When they returned to Terry's, Charlie couldn't get inside fast enough, leaving Herby to carry in the booze, and hoping there was really women there. There was, and so were a couple of mechanic friends that Terry worked with.

An hour later, about the time the pork chops were done, Trip showed up. Introductions were made, and the remainder of the evening went well. Ed ended up with a pretty blonde named Jackie, and they went with Herby and Trip to a motel where they all spent the night.

Meanwhile, Charlie made the same arrangement with Terry that Ed previously had, then Charlie and one of the other girls spent the night in Charlie's new bedroom.

About a week later, Trip was home helping her mom with dinner when her dad came home from work.

Jerry went to his room until dinner was ready, then Trip went in and said, "Hi Daddy."

"Hi Teri. How's my girl?"

"Uh . . . I'm good," she replied hesitatingly.

He looked up from his desk and asked, "What's on your mind, honey?"

"Remember all that I told you about my boyfriend?"

"Yeah," replied Jerry, pretending that he was only casually interested.

"Well . . .," and then Trip told him about Charlie.

"And these two guys can communicate with each other telepathically, huh?" Jerry asked casually.

"Yeah, I haven't seen them do it, but I know Herby well enough to know that he wouldn't lie, especially about something that has had such a profound affect on his life. He's even lost his family over it."

Trip and her father had a trusting relationship—that is, in the way that she could be open about her personal life without being judged.

"I believe you, Teri, and I believe that you believe him; furthermore, I believe that he believes it, but to elaborate any further on the reality of it right now, without proof, would only serve our imaginations. Ya know what I mean?"

"Yeah, I guess. I'm sworn to secrecy, anyway, so don't tell anybody, okay Daddy?"

"Your secret is safe with me."

CHAPTER ELEVEN

Bobby's Universe

In February, 1971, far away in Queensland, Australia, there was a man living in exile. Dr. Michael Denney had been a respected citizen there for the past twenty years. His exile was a result of his participation in mind control experiments performed on the Jews during the holocaust. He was a competent and respected member of the medical establishment, and his practice as a psychiatrist was above reproach.

The United States government captured and then set up Dr. Denney in Queensland, but his obligation to the United States government, in lieu of a prison sentence, would always be hanging over his head. He wasn't married and never had been, but his personal life *was*, however, within reproach, because of being a practicing bisexual and his patronage of the red light district. He was 65 years old, in good health, and had put World War II behind him without having to pay his debt to the United States - yet. That is; that by 1971 his time had finally come.

The United States government, as well as organized crime, was aware of anthros in Bobby's universe, but they hadn't, as yet, had the opportunities that presented themselves in Ed's universe.

Bobby's sister, Gerry, was a schoolteacher in Queensland. Before Bobby moved in with her, she got him a job in the maintenance department where she worked. He'd been there about six months, when walking the short distance from the school to Gerry's flat after work, a police car pulled up next to him. When the officer approached, he said, "You're under arrest for suspicion of bank robbery, Mr. Hickman." Then he was placed in the back seat of the patrol car. Bobby remembered how Herby handled a similar situation in Chicago, so he decided to do the same–he kept quiet. The police didn't bother with questioning, so he assumed that higher government authorities would do that eventually. Once he was placed in a cell, he summoned silently: "*Hey Herby*."

Herby and Trip were watching television when Herby heard Bobby's voice, but before he replied, he nudged her and said aloud, "Hey Trip, I'm about to have a silent conversation with an anthro right now."

"Really?" she replied, "Wow, I wish I could hear, but okay– go ahead, I won't interrupt."

"*Yeah Bobby*," was the reply as he focused on his fellow anthro.

"*You'll never guess what's happening to me right now?*"

"*You're probably right*," replied Herby, "*but not much surprises me anymore.*"

"*I guess you could say that I'm being legally kidnapped.*"

"*Oh yeah?*" said Herby as he gave Trip's leg a squeeze, "*as you know, I also went through that.*"

"*Yeah, Ed told me all about it, so I'm remaining silent like you did. Anyway, they got me for supposedly robbing a bank.*"

"*Bank robbery, huh? I didn't think you were the type,*" Herby replied in jest.

Bobby explained how it happened and then said, "*So here I am, a modern day John Dillinger.*"

"*Yeah, they have to make it a federal offense for jurisdiction purposes. That's what they arrested me for, too. Anyway, just bide your time, and the feds will be there to pick you up.*"

"*Okay*," Bobby replied as the sleeping old wino in his cell coughed, "*I'll keep you and Ed Posted.*"

"*Good. At least you're better prepared than I was when I*

went through all that shit."

Herby ended the conversation, then looked at Trip and said aloud, "Well what's it like to observe?

"You know how dead people look when their eyes are still open?"

"That's how I looked?"

"Yeah, it was eerie."

"Wow! None of us knew that. Hmm."

When the old wino on the other bunk began to stir, Bobby hoped he wouldn't have to talk to him; however, from previous arrests when he was a teenager, he knew that sometimes they could be entertaining conversationalists, but in this case, he figured that he'd have to breathe through his mouth to tolerate the stench of his filthy body, let alone the bad breath. Before the old wino could awaken completely, Bobby heard the jailer's keys jingling.

"Robert Hickman," the jailer announced. .

Bobby raised up from his bunk and replied, "Yeah."

"Come with me," the jailer commanded while unlocking the cell door. The next twenty minutes were spent taking finger prints and a mug shot, then he was returned to his cell.

"How ya doin young feller?"

"I'm okay, and you?"

"Oh, fair to middlin," replied the old man with a toothless smile. "What'cha in for?"

"Bank robbery."

"You don't look like no bank robber to me."

"What's a bank robber look like?" asked Bobby, not really wanting to make small talk.

The old man had to think on that momentarily. "I see your

157

point young feller," he replied as he got up to use the toilet. "How many banks have you robbed?"

Deciding that the old wino definitely wasn't the entertaining type, Bobby answered as politely as he could: "None sir, and if it's all the same to you, I'm gonna try to get some sleep now." He wasn't really sleepy, but that was the only way he could think of to get out of talking to him.

Every time Bobby heard the jingle of the jailer's keys, he hoped they were coming for him, but unfortunately, he shared the cell block with several other inmates.

About an hour later, he heard the keys again: "Robert Hickman."

"Yeah."

The jailer opened the cell door and said, "Come with me," and Bobby was led to an interrogation room where he waited for about five minutes.

When the door opened, a man in a suit entered and said, "Hello, Mr. Hickman, I'm agent Campbell, and this is my partner agent Raley."

Bobby just grinned with no intentions of saying anything.

Agent Campbell then said, "We're agents of the United States government." Then each of them presented their identification cards, and then added, "..and you're now going to be released into our custody."

Bobby continued grinning at them.

The agents looked at each other, and then agent Raley added, "Okay then, we'll see you when you're released."

An hour later Bobby was released into the agents' custody and taken to a nearby restaurant where they were to turn Bobby over to a local psychiatrist. When the doctor arrived, he sat down in the booth they occupied and said, "Good evening, my name is Dr. Michael Denney."

"My pleasure sir," replied agent Raley as they shook hands, "and this is Robeert Hickman," but when the doctor extended his hand, Bobby just sat there grinning.

"Mr. Hickman doesn't talk," said agent Campbell.

"Oh?" the doctor replied questioningly, and then added, "Well, hopefully I'll be able to change that."

When the agents left, the doctor said, "I don't have handcuffs Mr. Hickman, I'll just have to trust you." Dr. Denney suspected that there wasn't anything other than insolence keeping Bobby from speaking. The doctor hailed a cab, and directed the driver to Hill End, a suburb of Queensland. On the ride to the doctor's home and office, the old German thought about what he was instructed to do: experiment with this young man's mind with whatever methods he deemed necessary. Once they arrived at their destination, Dr. Denney prepared his young guest something to eat, made him as comfortable as possible, and then said, "I can sympathize with your reluctance to talk or cooperate, and you're probably wondering why you're here."

Bobby was hungry, so he ate voraciously, but his only response was a grin between bites.

"I'm really not sure myself," said the doctor, "all I was instructed to do is give you a physical and report my findings to the American authorities."

Bobby instinctively knew he was lying, and felt compelled to voice his opinion, but since he'd remained silent for this long, he wasn't going to take the shrewd doctor's bait. The food was spiked. An hour later, Bobby tossed and turned from what appeared to be a futile attempt at awakening from a nightmare, but Dr. Denney just watched the activity on the electroencephalograph (EEG) that was monitoring his sleep.

As he stood watching Bobby, he reflected back to his last month in Nazi Germany, and the mind control experiments he conducted. Presently he didn't find it necessary to resort to the methods that his previous superiors expected of him. He knew he'd have to pay for his protective exile eventually, but now that the time had come, he wondered how much longer he'd have to pay, and what it would entail. These same thoughts occupied his mind the week preceding Bobby's arrival when he was contacted by the American authorities, and required to attend a meeting concerning this obligation. He thought back to when he entered the American Embassy the preceding week, and a man about 65 years old with a conservative mustache and an aura of respectability approached with his hand extended, "Dr. Denney I presume?"

"Yes sir," replied the doctor.

"My name is Ignacio Sachs, and the United States government has chosen me to explain the dilemma we've encountered in which we need your help."

As they sat down, Dr. Denney replied, "My pleasure sir."

As Mr. Sachs got comfortable behind a desk, he said, "As you know, the time has come for you to donate your expertise. As far as I'm concerned, you could've gone the rest of your life without having to pay this debt that I personally feel wasn't really a debt owed in the first place, but that's just my opinion.

"Thank you sir."

"You have a successful practice, and you're a respected member of your community, so hopefully, you won't have to employ any of the methods of experimentation that were used under Hitler's regime, but in the name of national security—the United States security, of course, certain things have to be accomplished that don't appear to have anything to do with national security, so let me quit beating around the bush and get to the point. Doctor, uh . . . are you familiar with the term, anthropomorphic?"

"I'm familiar with Webster's defined," replied the doctor matter-of-factly.

"That's exactly where my knowledge lay when I was asked

160

the same question," said Mr. Sachs leaning forward in his chair, "Apparently, there's more to the definition than most people think. Anyway, soon, there'll be a young man brought to you for experimentation, and exploration of this phenomenon."

"Phenomenon?" asked the doctor.

"Yes, these so-called anthropomorphics are supposedly gifted with a preternatural phenomenon. We use the term preternatural, rather than supernatural, probably for the same reasons you have an obvious distaste for my use of the term, phenomenon."

"My distaste lies with experiments, sir. I didn't like doing them during the war and I'm not looking forward to doing them now," the doctor replied.

"My sentiments exactly, doctor; anyway, our government has documented proof, and other evidence that this phenomenon really does exist; however, we can't seem to hold on to one of these people once we have one in our custody."

"What do you mean by hold on?"

"Somehow, government agents manage to allow them to slip through their fingers without ever knowing how they got away, and we're talking about professional FBI agents here.

"Sounds rather anomalous, doesn't it?" asked the doctor while doing his best to appear intrigued.

"Very."

"What kind of a preternatural or supernatural syndrome are you talking about?"

"ESP, and there's evidence that they can manipulate animals and weather conditions; furthermore, as what happened with our government agents, they seem to be able to vanish, or disappear without anyone being able to account for or track them, especially when as many as twenty competent people were witnesses to it."

Still not convinced, Dr. Denney snickered and then asked, "So, before the eyes of all these people, these anthropomorphics can manipulate weather conditions, communicate with animals, have ESP, and can dematerialize at will? Come on sir, I . . ."

"Dr. Denney," Mr. Sachs interrupted, "I understand your skepticism, but the definition you're giving to anthropomorphic is the one that most people use, but check out this definition from a dictionary: *'the attribution of human motivation, characteristics, or behavior to inanimate objects, animals, or natural phenomena'*. The dictionary even uses the term, "phenomenon". Mr. Sachs then went on to explain what happened in Chicago with Herby, "..and a week after that," he added, "this young man was back home resuming his normal activities, just as though nothing happened."

"I see, so you want me to find out what makes this young man tick, is that right?" asked Dr. Denney.

"Yes sir, but you should know the method that has already been tried."

"What method?"

"Drugs and hypnosis."

"What kind of drugs?"

"One of the major syndicates of organized crime has also tampered with this; in fact, they administered Pentothal and performed hypnosis that eventually led to the incident that occurred in Chicago."

"I see. What does your government hope to accomplish by my findings?"

"I don't know,." Mr. Sachs admitted.

"I bet you don't?" Dr. Denney said accusingly. "I think both of us can read between the lines here, don't you?"

Without responding, Mr. Sachs asked, "Do we have your cooperation sir?"

162

"Yes, of course, but how am I to proceed with efficacy if I don't know what's intended for him?" the doctor probed.

"I don't know, but do the best you can for now, okay?"

"Very well," the doctor replied hesitatingly.

"I'll keep in touch, and hopefully I'll be able to provide you with more information."

Later, the doctor snapped out of his reverie just in time to notice his patient starting to stir with jerks and grunts. This was a subtle display that Bobby thought would be fun to alert the old man that he was coming to. He figured if he was going to be burdened with such incessant boredom, then he might as well play a few little games of his own.

Dr. Denney naturally assumed Bobby was asleep as a result of the drug that he spiked his food with.

While fighting sleep, Bobby thought about reporting what he was going through with one of his anthropomorphic counterparts, but decided against it for the time being.

Along with the jerks and grunts, the doctor noticed the activity on the EEG that was beginning to display mental activity.

Bobby was relatively sure of deceiving the doctor, but from his experience with EEGs when he was in the hospital, he wasn't so sure he could fool the graph. As it turned out, being capable of deceiving the machine, not unlike what yogis are capable of doing, was another subtle ability of anthros.

"Hello, young man," The doctor greeted as Bobby finally opened his eyes and performed a feigned yawn.

Of course Bobby was prepared not to be tricked into responding verbally, so he just looked at him and smiled.

"I bet you can talk if you wanted to," the doctor said while detaching the leads from the EEG, and then added, "If you're wondering what all these wires are for, I'll tell you." The doctor hesitated momentarily and then continued: "I've been monitoring your sleep to see if you have any sleep disturbances associated with neurosis. Your government wants to be sure you are of sound mind before your case goes to trial." The doctor was of course lying, and Bobby's expression reflected his suspicion of that.

A couple days elapsed, and the doctor made no progress whatever. To top things off, he hadn't yet felt any relief from the cold that he recently came down with. He dismissed it as not being long enough for the antibiotics he was taking to have taken effect. In his weakened condition, he couldn't help thinking of his clandestine activities in Nazi Germany. The doctor's examination room had a dead bolt on the door; furthermore, the rest of his home and office were burglar proofed, complete with bars over all the windows. With all this security, he naturally assumed that Bobby couldn't go anywhere. A couple days later he still wasn't over his cold, and he found himself procrastinating about the job he was supposed to do, so he eventually decided to try what had supposedly already been tried: Pentothal and hypnosis. He put Bobby under the influence of Pentothal, and then hypnotized him—at least he thought he'd hypnotized him because, in a way, he was the one that was hypnotized when Bobby froze him.

Now free to do as he pleased, Bobby started looking through desk drawers, dressers, and closets, anywhere there might be personal papers or documents that would provide information about the doctor. After a couple hours of searching, he found his birth certificate. Dr. Michael Denney was born in Frankfurt, Germany in 1900. Looking over the old document, an ominous thought occurred to him. Considering the doctor's age and birthplace, perhaps he was a former member of the Third Reich. Many Nazis escaped the Nuremburg trials and defected to various countries under assumed names; in fact, several of them were residing, incognito, in the United States, so why not Australia? He replaced the document and continued searching.

While going through an obviously unused closet, his suspicion was confirmed. There in the back, complete with moth balls, was a set of uniforms from Nazi Germany. Knowing that he could get away any time he chose to, Bobby wasn't scared, but he still wondered what this Nazi had in store for him. He didn't ransack the doctor's chest of drawers, but he did leave a few things, here and there, out of place to create suspicion upon himself. Just a little something more to irritate and confound him.

When Bobby returned to his stationary position, he released the doctor. The doctor's stationary position for the previous two hours left him a little sore and somewhat confused. He looked at his watch, stood up, rubbed his tush, and then did a double take on his watch. He checked the clock on his desk, and then sat back down. He searched Bobby's face for a glimmer of facial expression, but found none, just a grin. Observing the doctor's distress, it was all Bobby could do to keep from laughing. Now that he was starting to feel tired, it was fine with him when the doctor suggested that he lay down on the sofa and rest. Five minutes later he was asleep.

Meanwhile, when the doctor opened his desk drawer, his attention was drawn to a couple of items that were out of place. He kept his desk drawer locked while Bobby was there, and he hadn't noticed any damage caused by breaking in, so he dismissed it as something he had inadvertently done himself. About an hour later, when he was getting ready to walk to the local cafe and pick up something for him and Bobby to eat, he noticed the same type of disarray in his closet. He was able to disregard the desk drawer, but now he was impelled to examine the situation a little further.

"Anthropomorphic? ESP? Preternatural? Supernatural? Sorcery? Witchcraft? Psycho-kinesis? Poppycock!" he finally confirmed to himself. On the way home from the cafe, he realized what he needed to do, and this was not a very comforting thought, especially for Bobby. It was really

165

something that the doctor would rather not do. However, the thought that Bobby had been prowling through his house and office, eased his conscience somewhat, and then he thought of some of the old methods he employed in Nazi Germany. "Mr. Hickman," the doctor said as he shook Bobby's arm. "I've got some food here if you're hungry."

Forgetting where he was momentarily, Bobby opened his eyes, and there stood Doctor Denney glaring down at him, looking rather frustrated. The doctor couldn't figure out how Bobby could've gotten out of a locked office to go prowling through the rest of the house. Once Bobby was noticeably awake, the doctor turned around and left the room, leaving the food on an end table. Locking the door as he left, he then started checking other parts of his house to see what else might be tampered with.

It was obvious to Bobby that the doctor was suspicious, but he knew that the doctor's suspicion wasn't founded on proof, so he decided to confirm the doctor's suspicion. He thought how funny it would be to walk up to the doctor's front door and knock on it, and have the doctor find him standing there when he opened the door. This idea stimulated Bobby so much, that he started trying to figure out a way to do it, and then he did it.

When he was finished eating what the doctor brought home from the cafe, he went to use the rest room that was accessible from the office where he was held prisoner. When he was finished, he opened a curtain to the only window in the doctor's office. He peered out at the beautiful day watching and listening to the birds, and that's when the idea came to him. He thought about what Ed had once told him about his experience in the desert with getting a cow to help him. Then he thought how cool it would be if a bunch of those birds would come and peck at the weather beaten old plaster and cement that the bars that covered the window were imbedded in. It could've been a scene right out of Alfred Hitchcock's movie—*The Birds*. Bobby stood there mentally dictating the birds' actions. He kept them alternating,

166

so there wasn't so many at once, and to give their beaks a rest. This process continued incessantly for about an hour. When he heard the doctor's key unlocking the office door, he went over and closed the curtain, and at the same time he released the birds duties for the time being and made himself comfortable on the sofa.

"Young man," the doctor said to a smiling Bobby as he entered the room, "I know what you've been up to. I don't know how you've done it, but I just want you to know that I know!" and then he turned around and walked out again, locking the door behind him.

When the doctor was gone, Bobby returned to the window, pulled back the curtain, and summoned his little air force back again to peck away at the faltering old building. At that point it wouldn't be long before the birds' destruction would've served its purpose.

While the doctor was taking a shower, Bobby was climbing out of the office window. The birds were gone, having left the destruction of stucco, cement, and bars left on the ground. When Bobby walked around to the front door, he changed his mind about knocking on it. Since he'd been at the doctor's place, there'd been a lot of knocks on the door, and phone calls too, but the doctor didn't always answer them. His assignment with Bobby took priority, even over his medical practice, which convinced Bobby all the more that the doctor's intentions for Bobby were that of a sinister nature. He noticed a couple of lawn chairs and a picnic table in the front yard under a small canopy. As he made himself comfortable, he thought how nice it would be if he had a nice cold beer sitting in front of him. If nothing else, just to antagonize the doctor a little more, he considered leaving to get one, but decided against it. He didn't want to be gone when the doctor found that he was no longer in the house.

When the doctor finished his shower and got dressed, what he did couldn't have pleased Bobby more. When he opened his front door and looked outside, there was somebody sitting in his yard.

Bobby heard the door open, but for effect, he waited momentarily before he turned around, smiled, and said, "Hello Dr. Denney, beautiful day isn't it?"

The doctor was dumbfounded. His German white skin turned beet red, and his facial expression displayed his obvious rage. "How did you get out?" The doctor yelled.

Very composed, Bobby smiled and replied, "Calm down you old quack, take a Valium or something. You're gonna give yourself a heart attack. Now I want you to speak very nice to me, dick breath, because if you don't, I'll turn you into a toad."

The Doctor's outraged reaction reminded Bobby of Oliver Hardy when he was mad at Stanley. He then stormed back into the house. Bobby knew exactly where he was going, so he got up and went around to his escape window, and waited for the doctor to open the curtain. The doctor jerked open the curtain, and what did he see? Bobby, standing there smiling and waving his hand at him. The doctor pushed open the window and peered down at the destruction before him.

"What the hell?" The doctor said acrimoniously, "Come in here, young man, and explain this!"

"Have you bumped your fucking head, you deranged old creep. If I come in there, it'll be with a rock or a big stick." Bobby was tempted to reveal his knowledge of the doctor's past affiliation with the Third Reich, but he restrained himself.

Toning down the hostility in his voice in an attempt to reason with his adversary, the doctor said, "You can't get very far, the authorities will pick you up and . . ."

"I don't think so," Bobby replied with a smile on his face, "So catch me if you can," and he turned around and started walking down the street.

Doctor Denney's attempt at scare tactics wasn't effective; in fact, Bobby hadn't shown a glimmer of fear since he arrived. So, the doctor had unfortunately lost his patient. All he could do now was report what happened and hope there wouldn't be any recriminations.

Bobby borrowed money from his sister and caught the next flight back to the States. He figured there was no point in staying in Australia where he'd undoubtedly be harassed.

CHAPTER TWELVE

Jody

It was nearing the end of 1971, the year of Woodstock, and Bobby was back in Barstow living with his mother for the time being. Not having transportation for a job search, his mom drove him around looking for a car, and when he saw the old 55 Buick Special sitting on a back street with a for sale sign on it, he had to have it, so mom agreed to front the money as long as he paid her back as soon as possible.

His job search didn't take long, for he got his old job back at Denny's as a cook. He had a lot on his mind, still thinking about everything that happened in Australia. On his first day off, he decided to give the old Buick a road test, so he headed out of town on Highway 247 toward Big Bear. When he passed Barstow College, there was a guy around his age with his thumb out, so he stopped.

"How far are you going?" asked the hitchhiker after he got in and closed the door.

"Lucerne Valley, then I'm not sure. I'm just going for a ride. Where are you going?

"I haven't made up my mind."

Bobby stuck his hand out and said, "I'm Bobby Hickman."

"I'm Jody Byers, glad to meet you, and thanks for stopping. This didn't look to me like a very good place to hitchhike."

"It isn't, but you'll be alright when we get to Lucerne."

Jody agreed to accompany Bobby to the Victorville area before Bobby returned to Barstow. They stopped at a little market in Lucerne where Jody went in to get some beer. Prior to entering the store, a couple teenagers around 13 or 14 approached Jody. Because part of the building obscured Jody's view, he couldn't see the cop sitting across the street. Bobby did, however, and when he did, he said to himself emphatically: *Don't do it, Jody, there's a cop watching!*

For some reason, Jody looked around looking for a cop. He wondered if he was hearing voices because he was sure he heard a voice in his head that he wasn't inclined to ignore, so he said, "Sorry guys, I can't take the chance," and then he went into the store. When he got back into the car, he looked puzzled, then he noticed the police car. He looked over at Bobby, still wondering what the hell was going on, and then said, "Wow! you're not gonna believe what just happened."

While pulling out of the driveway, Bobby replied, "It looked to me like a couple kids asked you to buy them some beer or something."

"It ain't just that. I was gonna get it for em, but I heard a voice in my head warning me about that cop over there."

"Really? What exactly did the voice say?"

"Well . . . uh, it said . . . oh, it said, 'don't do it, Jody, there's a cop watching!'" and then he looked over at Bobby with that puzzled look on his face.

After hearing that, Bobby also had a puzzled look on his face. Sitting in silence for several seconds, Bobby looked over at him and asked, "Did the voice address you by name?"

Jody opened a couple beers, and when he handed one to Bobby, he replied, "Yeah, now that you mention it, but so what? Whether I was addressed by name or not, I clearly heard a voice telling me not to do it."

After taking a drink of his beer, Bobby asked, "And you've never experienced anything like this before, have you?"

"Fuck no, why do you think it's bothering me so much? Crazy people hear voices." They sat in silence again for a couple minutes, then Jody turned toward Bobby and asked, "Why did you ask me if that has ever happened before?"

Without looking at him, Bobby replied, "Because it happens to me."

"So you hear voices, huh?"

"Yeah, I do."

"Do you have a mental disorder?"

"No," replied Bobby with consternation, "but I, uh . . . hang on a minute, let me think . . .," and then he pulled into a gas station, parked, and then continued: "I've gotta piss," and he got out of the car. He walked a few paces, stopped, turned around and went back, opened the door, and added, "Don't be surprised if it happens again," and then he smiled, and went to the restroom.

Bobby urinated, then silently said, *"When I said 'don't be surprised if it happens again,' I bet you didn't think it really would, and I'm sure you didn't think it would happen so soon, right?"*

"Whoa, what the fuck!" was Jody's audible response.

"I didn't want to do this while I was still in the car, so don't panic. Right now, I want you to concentrate on me before you try to communicate with me." Bobby left the rest room and started walking around out of Jody's sight. They practiced communicating until Jody had it down. When Bobby got back in the car, Jody said aloud, "I hope you can explain this better. What little you told me when we were practicing wasn't enough."

"You're lucky because I actually can explain it. I'm sure there's more people like us around, but most of them are unaware of their abilities. I imagine many of them go to their graves without ever having known. If I hadn't picked you up, you might've been one of those who never found out."

"Okay, but that doesn't explain anything."

173

"Alright. Are you at all familiar with quantum physics?"

"Not really," replied Jody after he took a drink of beer, "but what's that got to do with it?"

"I'm about to tell you, but you're gonna have to let me talk for awhile."

"Okay, I'm listening."

"Well . . ., first of all I'll give you an example of quantum weirdness. Do you know what subatomic particles are?"

"I remember learning something about em in school but I forgot."

"They're electrons, neutrons, protons, photons, leptons, and the like, and here's where some of the weirdness lies: a quantum particle can (1) be in two places at the same time, (2) doesn't exist until it is observed, (3) can travel from one place to another without going through the intervening space, (4) can influence other particles at a distance."

"And everything in the universe, including us, are made up of atoms where these particles are, right?" asked Jody while he opened two more beers.

"Right."

"I don't remember much, but I remember that, but that's about the extent of it."

"The question I have about that,' said Bobby, "is... if the micro world behaves like that, then does the macro world—the world we live in—behave like that too?"

"Yeah, wouldn't it be cool if we could be in two places at the same time?"

"Yeah, but I only told you that to give you an idea of how weird the quantum world is. What comes next is different. Okay, there's this experiment called the double-slit experiment. You might say this is the granddaddy of quantum weirdness, experimentally, that is. Anyway, think of a movie screen, but

174

much smaller, with a piece of cardboard in front of it that has a slit cut into it."

"I thought you said this was a double slit experiment?"

"I did, but first we're dealing with one slit. Okay, imagine shooting particles or little balls of matter through one slit. On the screen behind it, we see a pattern in the same shape as the slit. That's what we'd expect to see, right?"

"Right."

"Now, if we add a second slit and do the same thing, we'll see two parallel patterns on the screen as we'd expect, right?

"Right."

"Now, let's consider waves rather than matter. When waves are projected through just one slit, there's a similar pattern but the band is a little wider, but when we add the second slit, something different happens: after shooting waves through two slits, there's an interference pattern like what would happen by dropping two stones in the water next to each other–the waves spread out and interfere with each other. So, on the screen, we see the interference pattern as a spread-out row of bands. Now, let's consider quantumly: think of an electron as a ball of matter like a little marble. If we fire a stream of them through one slit, it behaves the same way as before–a single band. Now, if we then shoot this stream of marbles through two slits, we'd expect two bands, right?"

"Right."

"Wrong. That doesn't happen. Instead, we get an interference pattern like what the waves produced. This doesn't make sense, so we think that maybe those little balls of matter are bouncing off each other to make that pattern. So, now we start shooting electrons through the slits one at a time over a period of time, and by doing this, there's no way they can interfere with each other. But, after an hour of this, we still see the same interference pattern. Our conclusion is that the single electron leaves as a particle, becomes a wave of potentials, goes through both slits, and interferes with itself. But mathematically it's even stranger: it goes through both slits and it goes through neither, and it goes through one and it goes through the other. All these possibilities are in superposition with each other."

"Wait, what's superposition?"

"It's a principle of quantum mechanics that holds that a physical system—such as an electron—exists partly in all its possible states simultaneously; but when measured or observed, it gives a result corresponding to only one of the possibilities. Did you get that?"

"It's a little confusing, but yeah, I think I get the gist of it."

"Okay, because we're so baffled by this, we decide to take a peek and see which one it actually goes through, so we put a measuring device beside the slits to see which one it goes through. When that's done, we think–WHAT? The damn electron went back to acting like a little marble, no more interference pattern! So, we have to conclude that the very act of measuring, or observing which slit it went through, meant that it only went through one, not both. It was as though the electron was aware that it was being watched. Hmm, we wonder what *are* these particles? Are they matter or are they waves? If they're waves, waves of what? And most of all, what does an observer have to do with it? We have to conclude that the observer collapsed the wave function simply by observing. And that's the dilemma of the double slit experiment. Now, remember the four things I mentioned at first about quantum weirdness?

"Yeah."

"Well, number two was that a subatomic particle doesn't exist until it is observed, and that observation or measurement is what collapsed the wave function and made a wave behave as a little ball of matter like a cue ball or marble. In other words, when you're not looking, it's a wave; when you're looking, it's a particle."

"Wow! and this is science and not science fiction?"

"The quantum world gets a lot weirder than that."

"And I bet you're gonna tell me how."

"Of course."

"Well, before you do, let's get some more beer."

"I've been so busy running my mouth," Ed replied, "I haven't finished this first one."

"Second one."

"Second one? Really. I don't remember the first one. Oh, there's a little market."

Back on the road toward Victorville, Ed continued. "Do you remember when I said that it's a principle of quantum mechanics that a subatomic particle, such as an electron, exists partly in all its possible states simultaneously?"

"Not really. All this stuff is new to me, but like I said, I think I'm following parts of it."

"That's okay. Anyway, a theoretical possibility or alternate theory for the collapse of the wave function is what is known as parallel universes. In 1957 a graduate student came up with the weird idea that physicists could take quantum weirdness seriously. So, if two alternatives can interfere with each other, then somehow those alternatives must both exist at the same time. And if possibilities can affect each other, like two or more probabilities adding up, then in some way these possibilities should really exist somewhere. The question is, where? Okay, in the double slit experiment, only two worlds were necessary. In one world, the particle passed through one slit. In the other world, the particle passed through the other. The two worlds would exist side-by-side, completely separate from each other until the particle reached the screen. Then the two worlds would overlap or merge. Are you following me so far?"

"I think so, go on."

"Okay. Uh, why would the two worlds merge after splitting apart? The answer was even more strange. The answer was self-consistency. This was the only way in which the interference could be explained and still have only one particle. The universe itself was continually doing this splitting and merging every time that anything interacted with anything else. Each split was necessary to produce the wave behavior and each merger was necessary to produce the particle. I realize all this is confusing, but stick with me. According to this explanation, the wave represents not possibilities or likelihoods, but realities–an infinite number of them. The wave is composed of particles in parallel worlds or universes. When the particle strikes the slits, the world, the whole universe containing it splits into two or a multiplicity of mutually unobservable but equally real worlds.

"Wow, you really know a lot about this."

"I didn't until I had to learn about it. Anyway, the metaverse, which is 'parallel universes' abbreviated, is described as an infinite series of existences, in a dizzily growing, ever spreading network of diverging, converging and parallel universes. This web of time–the strands of which approach one another, divide, intersect or ignore each other through the centuries–embraces every possibility. You see, we don't exist in most of them. In some you exist and I don't, while in others I exist and you don't, and in others both of us exist."

"All that you just said sounds to me like something out of a book."

"It is. I couldn't explain all this in my own words. I've read it over and over again, memorized it, so I could understand and repeat it verbatim."

"Okay, but what's all this got to do with me?"

"Well, you're alive in this universe and in probably thousands if not millions of others worlds, existences, or by whatever name you want to call them by. In this one, you have abilities like you and I experienced today. In others you don't, and there's no telling what other phenomenon is going on in others."

"You said abilities, plural. Did you use that word rhetorically or literally?"

Bobby lied when he said, "Rhetorically." He didn't want to give Jody too much of a sensory overload, plus he needed time for them to get better acquainted. By the time they returned to the Barstow area, they agreed that Jody should stick around for awhile, so Bobby talked his friend, Huck, into letting Jody move in with him for awhile. A month later, Bobby and Jody had become friends, with Jody being fully aware of his abilities. Ed, Bobby, Herby, Charlie, and now Jody kept in silent contact and tried to live their lives as simply as possible. Jody got a job as a gas pumper in a local service station. After both of them had been working for a month or so, they rented an apartment, agreeing not to use their abilities unless circumstances required it.

Bobby learned from a friend that his former girlfriend, Shirlee, was divorced and back in Barstow, so he called the number that his friend provided, and they talked for over an hour, catching up on each others lives. Bobby is only a memory to Shirlee in the universe where Bobby was killed in a car accident, but he's alive in another where they've rekindled their previous relationship.

In 1972, gas stations were actually *service* stations for two reasons: one, because service station attendants serviced cars by washing windshields, pumping the gas, and checking various fluid levels under the hood; two, because stations had lube bays where employees sold tires and accessories and did various types of mechanical work. In any area where tourists were prevalent, many of these service stations were owned and operated by unscrupulous men known as merchandisers. The con men who worked for these merchandisers were referred to as salesmen whose sales practices were scandalously unethical and illegal. Many salesmen were also known as fifty-percenters because they worked on a fifty percent commission. Fifty percent of the profit to the salesman and the other fifty percent to the merchandiser.

A couple months later, Bobby and Jody were sitting in Kelly's bar talking about Jody's work environment. "I'm working around a bunch of fucking crooks," said Jody.

"How's that?"

"The guys I work with trick customers into buying automotive parts they don't need."

"Like fan belts and radiator hoses and stuff?"

"No, like tires, shock absorbers, fuel pumps, fan clutches, batteries, and alternators."

"How do they trick them?"

"Well, one way is to squirt oil on one of the shocks while checking under the hood."

"You've seen em do this?

"Yeah, after they check the oil, they get down on their knees and reach under the car with a little squirt bottle in their hand, then get up and tell the customer they have an oil leak. The customer's are almost always concerned about an oil leak, especially when the attendant suggests that it might be brake fluid."

"Wow! And you've seen these squirt bottles?"

"Yeah, the salesmen–that's what they call themselves, don't pay any attention to me, they're too wrapped up with the con job."

"They'll eventually notice that you've seen them."

"They already have. One of them—the one called Dirty Dick, took me aside one day and asked if they could trust that I'd keep everything I see to myself."

"Of course you agreed?"

"Yeah, I looked at him like I was pissed off and said, 'Hey man, I ain't no fucking snitch,' and then I walked off."

"You think he was convinced?"

"I do. From then on—all of them, even the boss—started treating me like I was one of them."

"Wow! This is really fascinating. How do they go about all this?"

"Well, since they've come to trust me, I've been watching. For example, once the car is in the lube bay and up on the rack, the salesman pointed out to the customer that the seal on the front shock absorber had ruptured and was leaking hydraulic fluid. DD, that's ole Dirty Dick, then said, 'To save yourself a much higher repair bill later, sir, it would be wise to replace these shocks now. It doesn't matter where you buy them. You can get them at a parts store and install them yourself, or you can buy them at a department store where they're cheaper; but however you decide to do it, you'll be money ahead in the long run doing it as soon as possible—before any further damage is done.' Then DD explained what could happen to their vehicle if they continued to drive with it as it was."

"And customers generally go for it, right?"

"Oh yeah, when the customer asked if the work could be done there, DD quoted a price and told them that he could complete the installation within fifteen minutes, then assured them that the merchandise is guaranteed for the life of the car anywhere in the United States or Canada, as long as it's at one of their stations. This con job usually cost the customer hundreds of dollars by the time these salesmen are done with them."

"You said, one of their stations."

"Yeah, like a Mobil, 76, Shell, etc."

"They don't charge hundreds of dollars for a pair of shocks do they?" asked Bobby.

181

"No. When the fifteen minutes were almost up, DD walked into the lounge and said, 'Sir, would you come with me, please?'"

When DD brought the customer under the upraised car and pointed to one of the rear shocks, he said, 'Looky here, sir, it isn't as bad as the front one, but the leaking has started back here too."

"Another fifteen minutes for the rear ones, right?" asked Bobby.

"Yep, and because of DD's silver tongue, the customer sensed honesty and concern, and told him to install the rear ones too."

"That still doesn't add up to hundreds of dollars."

"Nope, at $33.95 a pair, plus labor, it's over a hundred dollars, but salesmen usually don't stop with just shocks or a fan clutch or fuel pump, or whatever else they might've brought them in for in the first place."

"Oh, I see. Once they get cars into the lube bay . . .."

"Yeah," Jody interrupted, "And they don't let them go until they've spent hundreds of dollars. Take DD for example; while he was installing the shocks, he evaluated the condition of the customer's tires. If the car was fairly new and the tires had less than six or eight thirty-seconds of rubber left on them, and they had a credit card, then they were also prime for a tire sale. Flaws and defects can easily be found on any tire, which can be exaggerated; however, why take the chance that the customer might not buy tires? Therefore, to insure that they do, these salesmen carry a small, sharpened, stubby type screwdriver, called a honker, which is used to cut the tire a little—just enough to show the cords on the inside of the rubber. They do this to two or three of the tires, and the result was generally the sale of a brand new set of tires."

"God damn! I'll never look at service stations the same way

182

again."

"Another approach to selling tires is on the island when the motorists are gassing up. If a customer's car already had new shocks, then they obviously can't sell them new ones. Instead, they try selling them something else. In their pockets, along with their squirt bottle and honker, they carry another devious little tool called a pinner. The pinner is also a small screwdriver, but not the stubby kind, the kind that fits into their shirt pockets along with a pen and a tire guage. This little screwdriver was sharpened like a pin to poke small holes in the tire. They don't pin tires on the island while they're getting gas, because if they don't agree to bring their car into the lube bay, then the customer will leave and have a flat down the road. Most of them couldn't give a shit whether they have a flat, but salesmen need to make every attempt not to get customer complaints. The oil companies will put the merchandiser out of business if they get too many. Anyway, after checking under the hood, they'll grab the air hose and pretend to air up the front, driver side tire. While they're doing this, they'll look up at the customer, and say that the tire only has about ten or fifteen pounds of air in it. This is usually cause for alarm, so the salesman offers to pull the car into the lube bay and check it at no cost. They tell the customer that if there's nothing wrong with the tire, then they could safely go on their way. If there was, however, then it would cost them to repair or replace the tire. Well, while the salesman is adjusting the racks—preparing to raise up the vehicle–they'll pin one of their tires and honk two others. The stage was then set for a tire sale."

"Wow!" said Bobby, "Makes ya wonder if all service stations are doing shit like that."

"It's done in primarily tourist areas like Barstow and Las Vegas. These guys I'm working with come from Las Cruces, New Mexico, so it's undoubtedly going on everywhere people gas up while traveling."

"What a bunch of fucking scumbags."

"Yeah, and depending on how convinced, and how willing customers are with parting with their money, is whether they'll continue to sell the customer automotive parts and accessories. Another major criteria for how far they'll push it, depends on how unscrupulous or money-hungry the owner of the station is. If the merchandiser don't care what lengths the salesmen go to for sales, then the sky is the limit and the salesmen continue to drain the customer. However, if the owner wants to stay in business for awhile, then he needs to avoid customer complaints, therefore deceitful or fraudulent sales tactics would be limited or prohibited. Anyway, by the time the customer rolls out of the driveway, they're usually happy and grateful that the condition of their vehicle was brought to their attention and taken care of so efficiently. To break down on the highway would be, to say the least, undesirable; therefore, service stations and their bright and friendly attendant's are often thought of as saviors."

"Yeah, sheep in wolves' clothing."

"Exactly, but sometimes these customers don't even have to be *sold*. Just mentioning that something is wrong is enough to persuade the customer to repair or replace whatever the vehicle needs. It's not uncommon for a customer to say, 'Okay sir, whatever you think the car needs, just put it on or fix it. We have a credit card and we don't want to have any trouble on the road.'"

"What an amazing story. Sinister, yet interesting."

"Yeah, with customers so willing to part with their money, salesmen are all too willing to keep taking it. So, after four shocks and a set of tires, these guys will often replace various other parts such as fan clutches, batteries, alternators, and fuel pumps. Usually though, it's one of those parts that they'll sell first to get them into the lube bay. Furthermore, these merchandising stations usually stock all the parts. When they don't have a part in stock, it takes only minutes to have them delivered from a part's warehouse, or they borrow them from another nearby merchandiser."

"Are you comfortable working with these fucking scumbags?"

"Not really, but it's interesting to learn about the ways of the world. It's a form of education, and like you said—a sinister one, but still an education. To give you an idea just how despicable they can be, listen to this. An elderly lady pulled into the station one day. DD lured her into the lube bay and up on the rack by one means or another, I don't know which, but without letting her out of the car. Once the car was in the air, a few minutes later he informed her that she needed four tires, and that to let her down and allow her to drive away would be endangering her and the lives of others on the highway."

"Let me guess: he wouldn't let her down until she bought a full set of tires?"

"Yes. Obviously, my boss don't care what lengths his salesmen go to."

"Then your boss is as despicable as the salesmen."

"Oh yeah, he was a salesman before buying the station. Being savagely unscrupulous is one end of the spectrum of this business, whereas the other end of the spectrum is legitimacy, and that end of the spectrum are usually local stations that cater to local customers–stations that aren't located where travelers gas up."

"Well, the way I see it, we can't do anything about it on a large geographic scale, but we can do things that'll appear to them as bad luck."

Jody knew exactly what Bobby was talking about. They then looked at each other and started laughing. "I think this is going to be fun," replied Jody.

"I think you're right."

CHAPTER THIRTEEN

Lube Bay Bandits

For the next month, Jody observed—getting more familiar with operations at work. He and Bobby discussed all the possible ways to interfere without arousing suspicion, then one day Jody decided to try something. There were two salesmen on duty, and whichever one gets to a customer first gets the sale. This time it was ole Dirty Dick. As DD approached the car on the island, Jody also approached a local customer. Being in close proximity to DD's customer, Jody saw DD take a grease rag out of the back pocket of his trousers, and at the same time withdrawing something out of his front pocket. With his grease rag still in his hand, he asked the customer for his gas order. After starting the gas, he went to the front of the vehicle and raised the hood. After he checked the oil, he got down on his knees, reached under the car, and squirted some oil on one of the shock absorbers with the little squirt bottle he had hidden in his grease rag. He then got up, went to the driver, and said, "Sir, you have oil leaking under your car."

The customer replied questioningly, "Oil?" Then he got out of his car and added, "Let me see." When DD brought him to the front of the car, he knelt down and pointed at the little puddle of oil. "What kind of oil is it?" asked the customer, becoming concerned.

"I don't know, but if it's brake fluid, I suggest you bring it into the lube bay and have us check it out." While DD was saying that, Jody was checking the oil on his customer's car. At the same time he concentrated intensely, visualizing DD dropping the squirt bottle in front of the customer.

Before the customer could respond to what DD suggested,

the squirt bottle slipped out of the grease rag and dropped on the island right in front of the customer. "What's that?" asked the customer.

After picking up the squirt bottle and slipping it back into his pocket, he replied, "Oh, just a lubricant for servicing cars. Anyway, would you like for us to check out that oil leak for you?"

The customer looked at DD suspiciously, then replied, "No, just top off the gas and I'll be on my way," and the customer got back into his car.

After the customer paid for the gas with his credit card and drove away, Jody smiled as DD walked back to the station's lounge area practically yelling, "FUCK, OF ALL THE GOD-DAMN LUCK! SON OF A FUCKING BITCH!"

When DD entered the lounge, the other salesman—Fred LaPoint, asked, "What's the matter, did you fuck up another sale?"

"I don't wanna talk about it," replied DD, not wanting him or anyone else to know just how bad he really screwed up.

There's no harm done if the customer writes a letter of complaint to the station owner, but a written complaint to the oil company is another matter. After so many of those, the station owner can get thrown out of the station. Merchandisers don't stay in business long, usually from two to four years, depending on how unscrupulously sales are handled, but during that time, they make a lot of money.

Jody forced the smile from his face when he walked into the lounge. There was no conversation going on and DD was mumbling to himself, obviously disturbed over his clumsiness.

* * * *

The apartment Jody and Bobby shared was on the side of a hill, which is the reason the white rocks on the hill above the

188

apartments are arranged to spell Hillside Apartments. When Jody arrived home, he explained what happened at work, and then they discussed other tactics Jody could employ to make things difficult for these lube bay bandits.

* * * *

The next day in the station lounge, when business was slow, Jody was talking with his unscrupulous co-workers. After having been their gas pumper for a couple months, they liked him and trusted him enough to discuss their unethical sales practices with him in the room. Fred asked Jody, "You don't seem to be interested in learning this business."

"No, but not because I don't approve of what you're doing."

"Why then?"

"Because I'm in the construction business, and the only reason I'm here is because there's no work available right now. I'm drawing unemployment and supplementing it with this job. As soon as construction picks up, I'll be leaving."

"So Dick, our venerable boss, is paying you under the table?"

"Yes."

"That makes sense."

Looking at DD, Jody asked, "Now that I've told you guys that, would you do me a favor?"

"Probably, what is it?" replied DD with a question.

"Don't tell Dick. I led him to believe that I needed a permanent job. If I woulda told him what I just told you, he wouldn't have hired me."

"How did you get him to pay you under the table?"

"Because I'm drawing unemployment."

"Oh yeah, you just said that. No problem, Jody," replied Fred, "Your secret is safe with us, at least it is with me."

"Me too," added DD.

After chatting for another twenty minutes, a local customer pulled in for gas. If customers weren't traveling, then it was the gas pumper's job to wait on them. It's only these corrupt merchandising stations that operate this way.

As Jody was entering the lounge after waiting on his customer, Fred was on his way to a car with Oregon plates. Sometimes he and DD would take turns, but that's usually not the case. Usually it's whoever gets to the customer first. After washing the windshield and looking under the hood, Fred grabbed the air hose and made it appear as though he was putting air in the tire. "This tire was almost flat, sir."

"Really?"

"Yeah, it only had about ten pounds of air in it," replied Fred as he got up and went back to top off the gas. After replacing the gas cap, Fred said, "If you like, we can put it on the rack and check for a leak. It won't cost you anything unless we have to fix it."

The customer handed over his credit card and replied, "Here, let me pay for the gas first. While the customer was signing for his purchase, Fred asked, "Should we pull it in and check it out? It might save you from getting a flat down the road."

While Fred was saying that, the customer heard a voice in his head saying, *"Don't do it. Start your car and get out of there."* The customer handed the signed document back to Fred and replied, "No, but thanks anyway," and then started his car and drove away.

To keep DD from noticing the smile that he couldn't seem to wipe off his face, Jody excused himself to go to the rest room. When he entered the room, he covered his mouth to keep from laughing and said to himself, *"Great! This is fun."*

When Jody walked back into the lounge, he heard DD say to an obviously bummed out Fred, "What's the matter, did you

190

fuck up another sale?"

"I don't wanna talk about it."

Customers from Washington and Oregon are referred to as cherries. They're almost always ripe for picking. If a salesman screws up a sale to a cherry when there's a fellow salesman around, he's ridiculed for it. For whatever reason, people from those states, and Canada, are the best targets for those in the merchandising business.

"You get to have all the fun," said Bobby.

"I don't see why you couldn't get in on it, too," replied Jody while channel surfing with the remote.

"How?"

"There's a coffee shop next door with booths right next to a window. I can see the people sitting in those booths from the station."

"Oh, I see. You could give me some type of signal and I could do a little mental manipulating from there."

"Yeah, why not?"

"Thanks for the offer, but there's a little too much room for error. No, keep doing what you're doing. Just hearing about your adventures is entertaining enough for me."

"Okay, but if you feel the urge, let me know and we'll give it a try."

After discussing more possible scenarios, Jody arrived at work the next day, eager to mess with the salesmen's minds. As it turned out, an opportunity arose that didn't come up in conversation the previous night with Bobby. While Jody was watching DD get ready to squirt a shock, a police car pulled in the driveway. DD delayed his next move, but the police officer stopped and appeared to be watching. He was watching, because Jody's telepathic suggestion worked: the officer heard a voice in his head suggesting that he stop and observe the station attendant. *That was weird*, the cop thought to himself after watching the customer drive away, *was that intuition or really a voice in my head?*

"Tough break Dirty Dick, looked to me like you had a real cherry there," said Fred when DD entered the lounge.

"Can you believe it? That fucking cop was watching me. I couldn't put it off any longer. That sale could have made my day."

While this conversation was going on, Jody noticed Bobby walking from the parking lot toward the coffee shop. Jody then asked, "Hey, would you guys mind if I went over to the coffee shop for a few minutes? My roommate just went in there."

"Go ahead, we'll cover for ya."

"Thanks."

After Jody explained what just happened, Bobby said, "I wonder if you could come up with a way to get those fucking crooks kicked out of there."

"There's no harm in speculating, but it'd be like killing one fly in a pig pen."

"Just how widespread is it?"

"Fred and DD told me that wherever there's people traveling, there are merchandisers. DD said he's worked in stations all through California, Arizona, New Mexico, and Texas. Fred said he's worked in several of them in California and Nevada. Barstow is ideal because so many highways start and intersect here, plus he's worked in Victorville and Baker. He also worked Interstate 5 between Los Angeles and Bakersfield in the Newhall / Saugus area and further up on the grapevine. And then there's Las Vegas, both of them have worked the strip and North Las Vegas. Those are just some of the areas where they've worked, so you can imagine how much more widespread it is. Shit, there's no reason to think that it's not in every State in the Union."

"I think you're right, but that doesn't mean we shouldn't at least try to put a stop to it here."

"Well, I'm glad it's fun, and I'm sure we'll come up with something."

A few days passed before Jody had another opportunity. Fred had to take the day off, so DD had all the potential sales to himself. On this sunny afternoon, a little ole lady with Washington plates pulled onto the island for gas. The greedy look on DD's face when he saw her, pissed Jody off. When DD practically leaped out of his chair to go hit this poor old woman, Jody's being pissed off turned into rage. Angry as he was, he decided to wait until he cooled off before he interfered, not wanting to take any chances of screwing it up. By the time Jody cooled off, DD had already low-tired her on the island and had her car on the rack with her in it. Jody had witnessed this deplorable tactic before. What made it so deplorable, is that DD wouldn't let the woman down until four new tires were mounted on the car. This time, like before, DD told her that he was unable, in all good conscience, to allow her to drive away on tires so defective that they would put her life and the lives of others in danger. In other words, he wasn't going to let her down off the rack until she bought four new tires. Jody kicked himself for not intervening before DD got her on the rack. There was nothing he could do. If he interfered with the tire sale, then she would drive away with the damage that DD inflicted on her tires, then she really would endanger herself and the lives of others on the road. The only thing Jody could think of to do was suggest telepathically that she take the old tires with her and have them checked later. That's what she did, and the end result was a nasty customer complaint. The station owner was given an ultimatum by Mobil Oil: fire the salesman or lose the station. Dirty Dick was fired, but not before he stuck it to several more customers, which Jody wasn't able to do anything about.

* * * *

Hanging around listening to the radio at their apartment, Bobby asked, "Who'd think that we'd ever have a white Christmas in Barstow?"

"I wouldn't have. I didn't think it snowed in the desert," replied Jody after taking a drink of soda.

"It usually doesn't. I've only seen it snow here once and that was when I was in the seventh grade. Since Jody moved out of Huck's place and started sharing an apartment with Bobby, they could speak freely about their anthropomorphic abilities. After a couple minutes, Bobby broke the silence: "I just thought of something: anthros have the ability to view what's going on in parallel universes, and this can be accomplished in a dream state by concentrating on a location prior to going to sleep at night. It can be done during the day, but we can screw up our sleeping schedule by forcing ourselves to do it during the day. Anyway, communicating with normal people in parallel universes isn't possible–just viewing them is, kinda like watching television."

"Have you done it before?"

"I have. I found out how to do it from my grandmother. She's an anthro too. Without her, I wouldn't know as much as I do; in fact, without her, I probably wouldn't know I had any abilities."

"You've never mentioned her before."

"I'm mentioning her now. Anyway, I did it when Ed and Huck were in Tijuana. They were helping out a friend down there, so when Ed contacted me, all I needed to do was practice, and after about a week, I was watching someone in San Diego while in a dream state in Barstow."

"Wow! This anthropomorphic shit gets more and more fascinating. Do we have more abilities that we're not aware of?"

"Probably," replied Bobby. "Like I said before, some anthros probably live their entire lives without ever becoming aware of their abilities."

"I can see how that could happen. If you hadn't connected

194

with me telepathically, I might not have ever known. Hmm, interesting."

"Yeah," replied Bobby, "So here's what I'm thinking: first, I'll find out who Ed needs to spy on – that is, whoever has the power to get merchandisers thrown out of stations."

"Good idea. Rather than focusing on salesmen, we could get that crooked fucking station owner kicked out. Who knows, maybe we can even get something done on a national level."

"Definitely something to think about," replied Bobby, "But first things first."

* * * *

About a week later, Bobby and Jody were having a beer at the Maya Inn. "Check it out," said Bobby after the bartender served them two beers, "In 1955, Socony-Vacuum was renamed Socony Mobil Oil Company. In 1963, it changed its trade name from Mobilgas to simply Mobil. There's more history that goes back to 1911, but there's no point in going into all that. Anyway, I found out that William P. Tavoulareas is President of the Mobil Corporation, so that's who I'm gonna have Ed watch from his existence."

"That should do it."

* * * *

"*Hey Ed.*"

"*Yeah, how's it going?*"

After taking a drink of his beer, Bobby replied, "*Not bad, but we do have something that we could use your help with.*

With Jody sitting beside him and listening to the conversation, Ed said, "*Okay, let's hear it.*"

"*Remember what I was able to do for you and Huck when*

195

you guys were in Tijuana?"

"You mean when you spied on that counterfeiter for us?"

"Yeah."

"Well, we need you to do the same thing."

"Alright, who and where?"

"We need to know where I can find William P. Tavoulareas, the president of Mobil Oil."

"Damn, you guys are messing around in the big leagues."

"Not really. I just need to influence him telepathically to do something that'll result in a crooked service station owner getting kicked out of his station."

"Oh," replied Ed. When Bobby explained everything that was going on in the Mobil station where Jody worked, Ed said, *"okay, when I find him I'll let you know his schedule so you can do your thing. However, be prepared for the possibility that this guy might not be president of Mobil Oil in my universe; he might not even be in my universe. If that turns out to be the case, then I'll monitor whoever is that's in charge and you can deal with him."*

"Sounds good."

Because of Jody's interference, salesmen continued having what they thought was bad luck. As a result, sales were down, but Jody couldn't be there 24/7 to thwart sales, so he did what he could while he was there. While Ed was looking into the workings of Mobil Oil at the corporate level, he was also in contact with Jody to learn about the various ways that customers were being cheated at service stations. Of course he was just as appalled as Bobby and Jody.

How convenient it would've been if Ed had the Internet to do his research with, but in 1972 he had to get information any way he could during his off hours from work. Three months later, however, Ed silently said, *"Hey Jody."*

196

"Yeah. I'm guessing you found out something."

"I have, but right now give me a minute to get Bobby on board with us here. I don't want to repeat all of this to him."

"Hey Bobby."

"Yeah."

"I found the man you guys are looking for, and it's the same William P. Tavoulareas that's in your existence."

"Where's he at," asked Bobby.

"New York."

"Shit!" replied Bobby, *"I don't have the money to travel that far."*

"No you don't," interjected Jody, *"but I think my scoundrel of a boss could afford to lose some money in a robbery."*

"I don't think you guys should start committing felonies," replied Ed, *"there's gotta be an easier way."*

"Right now, my boss is short of help," said Jody, *"and because of that, I'm working one graveyard shift by myself. Ed, you can come by and get the money around three o'clock in the morning. I'll give you time to get home, then I'll call the police and give them a report describing the robber and the car he was driving."*

"It's still a felony," commented Bobby, *"but it's one that would be easy to get away with."*

"Our reasons justify it," confirmed Ed.

They all agreed, and a week later Bobby was on his way to New York, but first Ed sent a letter to Mr. Tavoulareas informing him of the unethical and illegal sales practices going on in a Mobil station in Barstow.

After arriving in New York, Bobby went to the recently built world trade center. Ed had told him that Mr. Tavoulareas could be found in the north tower. Having looked on the wall directory and found his way up to the 36th floor, Bobby waited for the man, whose picture was in his wallet, to leave his office. At 11:30, the man in the picture came out of his office and went to a nearby coffee shop. Bobby followed him in, took a seat, and waited until he ordered his lunch. After Bobby ordered something, he noticed Tavoulareas pick up a newspaper, but before the man started reading, Bobby telepathically caused him to lay down the newspaper and start thinking about the letter he received recently about unethical sales practices going on in California. He was reminded of other letters that he received periodically over the years. When he finished his lunch, he returned to his office and made a call to the California Department of Consumer Affairs. After that, he contacted Mike Wallace of 60 minutes and asked if he'd be interested in an expose. Tavoulareas told him that this affront to the American people has gone on long enough. Mr. Wallace concurred.

When Bobby observed these phone calls, he was satisfied that his purpose in going to New York was accomplished, and then some, so he did a little sight seeing, ending with a ride on the *Maid of the Mist*, where he had the overwhelming experience of Niagara Falls. The next morning, when he got on the road back to California, he silently said, *"Hey Jody."*

"Yeah, how's it going back there?"

"Mission accomplished, and even more so than we hoped."

"How's that?"

"Apparently, it's a job for the California Department of Consumer Affairs, rather than the police. Anyway, judging from my observations, I think you'll probably witness something soon. Just wait for it. I'll explain the rest later."

"Okay, see you when you get back."

* * * *

A week later, Jody watched Fred, the only remaining salesman, bring a woman with Canada license plates into the lube bay. Jody knew that when a canuck pulled onto the island, the sky was the limit when it came to how much pressure the salesman would apply for a sale. Canadians were preferred targets, even over travelers from Washington and Oregon. They were considered cherries—ripe for the picking. Jody was seething inside having to do nothing but watch, but Bobby told him not to interfere anymore for awhile. He was supposed to wait. This day, however, the waiting ended.

When the sale was finished, the woman had purchased four new tires and four new shocks. Jody was disgusted seeing the self-satisfied look on Fred's face when the woman pulled out of the lube bay. That self-satisfied look changed when Fred and Jody witnessed two official looking white cars with government license plates pull in next to the cherry canuck. Men in suits directed her to a parking space adjacent to the station where they all engaged in conversation. Then the men walked over to Fred and showed him their identification as agents for consumer affairs. Within the hour, the station was closed. The station had been set up–the agents had inspected the car before they sent the woman agent into the station. After the sale, they confiscated the old shocks and tires, which were in perfect condition except for the damage done to the tires by Fred. The cuts between the tread and on the sidewall of two tires weren't there when they inspected the car beforehand. The shocks weren't damaged, but there was oil on them. It was easy enough to conclude why.

Jody was released, but Fred was arrested. Since an arrest by consumer affairs isn't considered a criminal offense, he was also released on his own recognizance and given a court date in a civil court. Since the owner of the station stated that he had no knowledge of what Fred was doing, he was back in business the next day.

Although Jody was unemployed, or so he thought until he was called back to work the next day, he and Bobby celebrated their accomplishment that night, but there was more to the story

199

that Bobby didn't know yet. While drinking beer in their apartment, Bobby said, "You probably don't remember, but when I told you about what happened in New York, I said that I'd explain the rest later."

"The rest of what?" replied Jody.

"Mr. Tavoulareas made two phone calls. I only told you about one of them. The other one was to Mike Wallace."

"You mean the 60 Minutes guy?"

"Yep."

"How's that gonna work?" asked Jody.

"I don't know, but there'll probably be a nationwide investigation."

"Yeah, and they'll probably start with the California Department of Consumer Affairs."

"Probably, since they're the ones that caught them here."

"Yeah, and they'll probably furnish enough information about what happened here to continue the investigation."

"Wow! Maybe we really did something here."

"I think so."

CHAPTER FOURTEEN

Cheating the Cheaters

While sitting in the Foxfire Lounge, Herby took off his Lincoln/Mercury hat and said, "another strange thing happened to me today on my lunch hour."

"Don't tell me, you have x-ray vision," replied Trip jokingly.

"That would be nice, uh . . . ." Herby replied hesitatingly while thinking about the customer he'd left standing in the parts department, "Uh, anyway, I was sitting at a traffic signal and I noticed a little old lady walking down the side alley carrying a sack of groceries. She had a purse hanging from her arm, and behind her were two young thugs. I could tell what they were about to do, but I was powerless because I was stuck in traffic. About the time they made their move, I wished like hell the one in front would stumble, fall down, with the one behind him tripping over his accomplice. At precisely the time that I wished that . . . ."

Trip interrupted by saying, "..and it happened, right? Just like you wanted it to."

"Yeah. Yeah, it did, but I have a hard time believing that I had anything to do with it."

"Why not? This isn't the first time these types of things have happened to you, you know. Everything that happens don't always have logical explanations."

"I can't help thinking they do," Herby replied after taking a drink of his beer. "Uh . . . it's just that we're incapable of figuring out what they are."

"So, are you saying that you think what's been happening to you are just coincidences?" Trip asked as she delicately sipped her margarita.

"I don't know. I keep wondering if everybody has abilities that others don't. Some people sing really good; others are gifted at mathematics; I, however, can't do either one. So why couldn't it be the same with what me and my counterparts have somehow tapped into."

"Hmm, yeah, I can see how that might be possible."

"Well, thanks for taking me seriously. You see, you're the only one who knows me well enough for me to tell all of this to, without you thinking I've gone off the deep end."

Herby withheld the part about parallel universes thinking she had enough to process without going into all that, but when thinking about it, he thought about the discussion he once had with Ed about the possibility of there being many copies of ourselves in other universes, having abilities in one existence might not apply to others. In others, perhaps we have different abilities or none at all.

He and Trip made small talk for awhile and had another drink—not talking about the incident any further. Finally, Trip said, "I have to go. My dad wants me to help him at the sports book tonight."

"Gonna have somebody bumped off, huh?" Herby said jokingly.

"Yeah, right."

Herby laughed as they got up to leave and then said, "I also need to get home, my wife is probably home from her PTA meeting by now."

On their way to their cars, Herby said, "Let's meet here first when I get off tomorrow and then get a room, okay?"

Trip got into her car and closed the door. Herby bent over and gave her a kiss, and then she replied, "Okay, see you then."

When she entered her father's office at The Sports Book, she said, "Hi daddy."

"Hi honey."

Trip took a seat opposite him at his desk and said, "Remember what I've told you about my boyfriend?

"Yeah," Jerry replied, appearing as though he was preoccupied, "did something else happen?"

Trip explained what Herby said at the bar, and when she was done he replied, "All this is pretty hard to swallow, Teri, but you're convinced he's telling the truth, right?"

"I am, and the reason I am is because he's the type a guy who wouldn't believe it if someone told him something like this."

They talked casually for awhile, then Jerry said, "Well, I'm not gonna need you here tonight after all, but I appreciate you coming over, but there is something that you could do for me before you leave."

"Okay."

"Would you stop by the Tropicana Sports Book on your way home and pick up some racing forms? I'll bring them to work with me in the morning. There's enough here to last till then."

As Trip got up to leave she said, "Okay daddy, I'll see you at the house."

Jerry walked her out to the front counter and while standing by his employee, he watched her exit the building, get into her car, and drive away. He looked at the man beside him and said, "Joe, hold any calls I might get, and if anybody comes in asking for me, tell em I'm not here, okay?"

"Okay boss."

When Jerry returned to his office, he walked to the telephone and dialed a number.

The voice on the other answered, "Hello."

"Hey Big Head. Jerry here, in Vegas."

"Hey Jerry, how's it goin?"

"Can't complain. Is the all mighty hawk still kicking up back there?"

"You know it is, but you didn't call to talk about weather conditions in Chicago, so what's up?"

"Remember what I was telling you about my daughter's boyfriend?"

"Yeah, I'm all ears."

"Well, she told me something I think you'd like to hear."

After Jerry explained what Trip said about Herby, Big Head replied, "Really? Hmm, interesting . . . Should I arrange a meeting with that shrink in Vegas?"

"Yeah, I guess."

"Okay, I'll call you when it's set up."

"Sounds good. Be talkin to ya, eh."

Jerry hung up the phone and sat there thinking about hiring a couple guys to abduct Herby for him.

* * * *

Terry Russell, whose nick name was Crazy, and Richard Reeves were friends, both single, and both had drug and drinking habits which forced them to partake in criminal activity to supplement their incomes. Crazy was in his apartment watching television when the telephone rang."

"Is this Mr. Russell speaking?"

"Yes it is, Jerry, I recognize your voice."

"Good, good. Say kid, was wondering if you and your partner could be available within the next week or so?"

"I think so."

204

"Well, I'm not exactly sure when, but I wanted to make sure I could count on you guys."

"I don't think there'll be a problem. Give me a call when you're ready.

"Okay kid, be talkin' to ya, eh." The conversation ended and the only thing that was delaying Jerry's plan was a phone call from Chicago.

About a week later, Crazy and Richard were at the Lazy Bar saloon. Richard took a drink of beer and asked, "So, how much is Jerry going to pay us for risking a prison sentence?"

"That's a hell of a way to look at it," replied Crazy.

"It's true, isn't it?"

"I guess that depends on how careful we are."

"Anyway, how much is he paying us?" Richard asked again as he lit a cigarette.

It was quiet in the bar up till this time. Crazy had to raise his voice now that the juke-box started playing *Hey Jude*. "He didn't say. What difference does it make? He's always been fair, hasn't he? You're sure sniveling a lot. Want me to get someone else to help me do this or what?"

"No, I'll do it. I need the money, but I don't like doin' shit like this."

"Neither do I," replied Crazy.

"Well," said Richard as he finished his beer, "let's go check out where this Jim Matthews lives. It'd be our luck he's got a gang of security guards and a pack of killer dogs surrounding the place."

"Wa wa wa," replied Crazy as he got off the bar stool. "Let's go."

They left the bar and got into Crazy's old Dodge pick-up with a camper shell and drove to the address that Jerry gave

205

them. Herby lived on a corner lot, so Crazy and Richard parked on the cross street and waited. "I wonder how long we're gonna have to sit here waiting?" complained Richard.

"Quit whining, will you?"

They sat there about twenty minutes when they saw an old white 1960 Dodge Seneca pull up and park. Herby got out of his car and went into his house. "That's the guy," said Crazy, "he fits the same description that Jerry gave me. And you know what?"

"What?" replied Richard suspiciously.

"I think we can take care of this right here and now with that wall being there like it is."

"Yeah, we can hide behind it."

Just then Crazy opened his door and said, "Wait here, Richard. When you see his body go limp, come over and help me bring him back to the truck, okay?"

Fortunately, for them, they didn't have to wait long. Herby came walking out to his car, and when he was unlocking it, Crazy snuck up behind him and reached around his neck and placed a wet rag over his mouth. At first Herby struggled, but soon he unwillingly acquiesced when the chemical on the rag took affect. Richard was there to help get Herby into the bed of the truck. Once they got him in, they tied him up and gagged him. Then Richard said, "I'll stay back here, and if he starts to stir again, I'll put him out again."

"Okay," replied Crazy as he got out of the camper and closed the camper shell, "I'll drive down to the nearest phone and call Jerry."

"Hello."

"Is Mr. Galloway there?"

"Who shall I say is calling?"

"Terry Russell."

206

"Just a minute, please," replied Trip.

While Crazy waited for Dennis to come to the phone, he said to himself, *what a sweet sounding voice. I wonder who that was.*

Jerry came to the phone and asked, "Yeah Crazy, do you have something for me?"

"I do."

"Okay, give me the number that you're calling from, and I'll give you a call back in a few minutes."

Crazy gave him the number and Jerry said, "Got it. I'll call ya shortly."

While Crazy was explaining to Richard what was happening, there was another telephone conversation in progress.

"Hello," answered Dr. Lloyd.

"Hi Doc. My name is Jerry Galloway, I believe you've been expecting a call from me."

"Yes sir, I have. Do you have something for me?"

"I do."

"Can you bring it to my office?"

"Yes," replied Jerry.

Crazy and Richard were talking through the camper shell window when the pay phone started ringing. Crazy ran over and picked it up: "Hello."

They agreed where they were to meet and then said, "Okay kid, be there in about ten minutes."

Their rendezvous was on a back street close to the psychologist's office. When Jerry pulled up to the back of the truck, Crazy went to Jerry's window and asked, "Now what?"

"Put him in my back seat and I'll take care of the rest."

Once Herby was placed in Jerry's car, Jerry started his car and said, "Come by The Sports Book anytime tomorrow, and I'll pay you. As he was pulling away he said, "Be talkin' to ya, eh."

After Herby was placed in Jerry's back seat, the guys returned to Crazy's old truck and left.

Jerry pulled up to the rear entrance of the doctor's office and turned off his lights and motor. As he opened his car door, the back door of the doctor's office opened, and a man of about 50 years with salt and pepper hair stepped out. When the man approached Jerry he said, "Dr. Lloyd, pleased to meet you, sir."

Jerry grabbed the doctor's outreached hand and replied, "Jerry Galloway, it's my pleasure, sir."

The doctor helped Jerry get Herby inside, and they positioned him comfortably on a sofa, then the doctor motioned for Jerry to have a seat and said, "Make yourself comfortable Mr. Galloway, but before we proceed, we need to establish our positions here."

"I like your style, doc. No sense leaving any room for misunderstandings, right?"

"Yes," the doctor replied, "So I must insist on one thing before we go any further. My technique in hypnosis is my own and unknown to anyone other than myself, so when I do this, I can't allow anybody to witness my procedure."

"I understand doc. So . . . you won't mind if I do my thing with him without you in the room. Is that okay?"

"Of course," agreed the doctor. "Now, the first voice he'll be aware of when I release him, will be yours; furthermore, it'll be the only voice that he'll adhere to thereafter. When your voice addresses him by his first name, which is Jim, that's when he'll be under your control. At that point the stage is set for you to call the shots. First though, I think I should offer you some suggestions on how best to manage him."

Jerry remained silent and listened attentively.

"It's imperative to be polite, sir." The doctor hesitated and held eye contact with Jerry momentarily before continuing. "It appears to me that you're a naturally nice fella."

208

"It doesn't cost a thing to be nice, doc."

"You're quite right. Now, I'm sure you've heard that when a person is under hypnosis he won't do anything asked of him that he wouldn't ordinarily do had he not been under the influence."

Herby started to stir, and the doctor casually got up and went to a cupboard and prepared an injection and said, "A mild short-acting sedative," as if he were justifying his action.

"Anyway," the doctor continued, "that's a basic generality; however, I'm sure you're familiar with manipulative psychological questioning to avoid that rule of thumb, such as: indirect questioning, making statements in question form, vice versa, and so on. Is that right, sir?"

"Yes, of course. I'm aware that the interrogative process will have to be treated delicately," Jerry confirmed.

"My only real concern is that no harm comes to this young man."

Starting to get irritated, Jerry replied, "Yes, of course, doc."

Jerry left the room while Herby was being hypnotized. When he was finished, he summoned Jerry back to the room and was awarded with a smile and a nod, and then the doctor left the room.

Jerry took a seat on a stool next to where Herby was sitting and said, "Jim, if I say anything that you're not comfortable with, feel free to state your concern, okay?"

"Okay," replied Herby complacently.

"How are you today, Jim?"

"I'm okay, sir," Herby replied, making direct eye contact.

"You don't have to address me as sir, Jim. Think of me as your friend and call me Jerry, okay?"

"Okay, Jerry."

"It would be great if there could be a way to rid our city of thugs and drug addicts and other criminals, wouldn't it, Jim?"

"Of course," Herby responded with a slight smile, appearing to be pleased with himself.

After some small talk, Jerry started feeling a little more confident now that Herby appeared to be relaxing and agreeing with him somewhat, but he wondered why Herby had appeared to be pleased with himself when he answered that last question.

"You appear amused, Jim. Is there any particular reason why?"

"Yes."

Jerry smiled and then asked, "Would you have any objection to telling me what amused you?"

"No." Herby replied without elaborating.

That short answer annoyed Jerry, but he really didn't know why; however, after a moment's thought, he realized that he should have phrased the question differently. "Would you please explain why you were so amused by that question?"

"It was an experience I had the other day concerning some thugs."

"What was that experience, Jim?"

As with Herby's explanation to Trip, he again repeated it for Jerry, and then smiled again as though he was pleased with himself.

"I see. So, how did you get the thugs to fall down like that, Jim?"

"I didn't," Herby replied firmly.

"Jim," Jerry said with polite authority, "You just told me that you wanted those thugs to fall down, and then they did. Isn't that right?"

"Yes."

After taking a deep breath, Jerry asked, "why?"

"Why what?"

"Why did you think you could make them fall down."

"I didn't," replied Herby, again acting pleased with himself.

"You didn't what, Jim?" Becoming exasperated, Jerry was starting to realize that his earlier satisfaction with Herby relaxing a little, was premature.

"I didn't think that I could make them fall down."

"Why not?"

Herby just looked at Jerry with an expression insinuating what a stupid question it was, and then didn't answer at all.

Jerry felt like he was spinning his wheels. Suppressing his frustration so not to alarm or upset Herby, he decided to call it a night so he wouldn't hinder any later attempt at interrogation. He began to sum up by saying, "Well, Jim, it's been nice chatting with you. I'd enjoy chatting with you again sometime." Jerry wanted to plant the seed in Herby's mind for a future session by saying, "Jim, anytime you hear my voice addressing you by your first name, I'd appreciate it if you'd give my request first priority at that time. Okay?"

"Okay."

"Remain sitting where you are, Jim, and I'll be right back."

Herby sat motionless with a slight smirk on his face that for some reason intimidated Jerry. He felt like grabbing Herby and choking the shit out of him, but he kept calm and returned to the doctor's office. As he walked in he drew a deep breath and looked at the doctor quizzically and said, "Doc, I'm finished for now. I assume I won't be needing your assistance to initiate any further interrogation, right?"

"No, but I must insist on being notified when you've finished with him, okay?"

"Of course."

"Here's one of my business cards Mr. Galloway, please call me if there are any complications, or if there is anything else I can do for you."

Tired and wanting to get home, Jerry asked, "Okay doc, how should I go about returning him?"

"Take him somewhere like a cocktail lounge, and buy him whatever he wants to drink. Then show him a clock, or inform him of the time. Then tell him that in exactly ten minutes, or when he finishes his drink, that he'll then return home with no knowledge or memory of what occurred."

* * * *

Herby looked at the clock that was in front of him and it read two-twenty. He didn't know whether it was A.M. or P.M., because he was inside of a bar, and Las Vegas bars stay open twenty-four hours. He looked around and then looked at the almost finished Budweiser that sat before him. He didn't remember ordering or drinking it. Then he looked at the bartender who just walked up.

"What's the matter with you, buddy? You don't look so good."

"How long have I been here?" Herby asked, feeling disoriented.

The bartender gave him a queer look and replied, "You don't know?"

"Do you know or not?" Herby asked indignantly.

The bartender gave Herby a salty look and then replied, "About fifteen minutes, pal."

With a dazed and confused expression on his face, Herby asked, "Did I come in here with anybody?"

The bartender looked at him as though he were nuts, but before he could answer, Herby asked, "Did you hear me? I asked...."

"I heard you," replied the bartender, getting more irritated. "You came in alone, pal," and then he walked off. The bartender lied. Jerry paid him to say that and to behave as he did.

Herby thought to himself, *I recognize this place. Damn, I have a headache. The last thing I re . . .* Herby then got off the bar stool and walked outside. Again, he thought to himself, *fuck that prick bartender. I wonder where my car is?* Being two o'clock in the morning, the weather was cool, so he started walking. He decided against mentioning any of this to his wife, since that would only serve to complicate matters. Then he thought about his car again: *Car . . . my car . . . that's the last thing I remember. I was unlocking my car, and getting ready to leave, and . . . Shit! That's it—until just a little while ago. It's as though I'd been asleep and just woke up in the bar.* He rounded the corner by his house and there sat his car. When he got inside the house, he lay down on the couch and thought, *I wonder if this has anything to do with the things that have been happening to me?*

Jerry was sitting in his office about three days later trying to come up with a plan for Herby. The information he'd come by originally concerning anthropomorphics, came from a reliable source of the underground world. This wasn't just idle gossip, theory, or folk lore. This was reality, and Jerry believed that he'd found an opportunity to manipulate it. If he was successful in this endeavor, he'd be respected by his peers.

Jerry picked up his phone and dialed a number.

"Hello."

"Hey Big Head?" Greeted Jerry while kicking back in his office chair.

"Yeah Jerry, what's new?

"Need to talk to ya."

"Can it wait till tomorrow? I was just leaving."

"What time?"

"Any time. I'll be home all day."

"Okay, be talkin' to ya, eh."

At noon the next day Jerry drove to Big Head's house in Henderson, Nevada. When he knocked on the door, a big blonde haired, blue eyed man answered and said, "Come on in."

Jerry followed Big Head back to a study where they took a seat on a circular sofa with a coffee table in the middle.

"What's up? asked Big Head as he put his feet up on a coffee table.

Also putting his feet on the coffee table, Jerry replied, "I think I have discovered an avenue of entry into this anthropomorphic phenomenon."

Big Head looked at Jerry momentarily and said, "Uh huh."

"Listen! I didn't come all the way over here to make fucking jokes, damnit."

"Okay, okay, calm down, take a valium or something. Tell me what you have, I'm all ears."

"Do I have your undivided attention and support?"

"Yeah, yeah, spit it out. I never buy a pair of shoes until I've tried them on."

"Alright. First of all you need to find out if there is going to be any hits in this area in the very near future. If so, we need to arrange to have it done in the presence of somebody I have in mind."

"Why?"

"Because I think this person is anthropomorphic."

Big head responded to Jerry's last statement with guarded enthusiasm and then said, "I hope you know that our people have been experimenting with manipulation and control of these people for years, and to no avail I might add."

214

"I know that, but they haven't experimented with one that isn't aware of his abilities."

Big Head's eyes then widened and he said, "Ohhh. I see what you mean."

"Now, can we talk business?" asked Jerry.

"We certainly can. So, you think that by having this hit attempted with this guy witnessing it, he might use his ability, unknowingly, to prevent it, right?"

"Right."

"I see. So, we'd also need a dispensable hit man, too, just in case," suggested Big Head.

"Now you're getting the picture," said Jerry with a I-told-you-so look on his face.

"I'd like to watch this myself."

"Me too. I've already got this guy under hypnosis. All I have to do is summon him on the telephone. When he hears my voice, he's under my control.

"Well, I see you've been doing your homework. I'm definitely convinced that all of this has merit. So, you can depend on my full cooperation. I'll do everything I can to accommodate you."

"Okay, be talkin to ya, eh." Jerry said as he left.

* * * *

About a week after his loss of memory, Herby was working around his house. When he was mowing the lawn, his kids came running outside arguing, as siblings do. Herby straightened the situation out as best he could, and they returned to the house temporarily pacified. While trimming the bushes, he thought about calling Trip. They wasn't able to keep their previous date, and he hadn't talked to her since they were in the lounge, so he felt compelled to tell her about his memory loss.

215

Trip left The Sports Book about three o'clock on this same day. She'd been helping her father. Driving home, she also thought about calling Herby. She had until 4:30 to catch him before his wife arrived home from work.

"Hello," answered Herby, after about four rings.

"Hi honey," replied Trip, "why haven't you called me?"

"I've been intending to, because something else has happened, but I didn't want to bother you again with it."

"Herby, I don't mind at all. You should've called. Especially since we missed our date last week."

"You're right, I should've. What are you doing tonight?"

"Nothing. Why don't you meet me at that same cocktail lounge, say at seven, okay."

"Okay," replied Herby, "see you there."

Herby sat in his car in the parking lot of the cocktail lounge about five minutes before Trip pulled up. They both got out of their cars and went inside. They went to the bar, and as they were taking a seat, the bartender walked up and said, "Good evening, pick your poison."

"I'll have a beer, and she'll have a margarita."

When they received their drinks, they moved to a booth and took a seat beside each other. "I think I might have Alzheimer's disease," Herby said jokingly.

"Of course you do. Alzheimer's at 25," Trip replied after thanking the bartender for bringing the drinks.

Herby explained his experience, and when he finished she looked at him and said jokingly, "Maybe you do have Alzheimer's disease."

Herby laughed and replied, "I'd much rather joke about all this than to let it get to me."

"I don't know how you keep it from getting to you. I'd be a

216

basket case if all this were happening to me."

Herby raised his eyebrows and said, "Where would you like to shack up for the night?"

"Shack up?" she asked, offended like, "That sounds so cheap. How about spending the night together?"

Herby shook his head and replied, "Semantics. Okay, let's go."

They left the lounge without finishing their drinks and spent the night in a motel.

* * * *

Early Sunday morning at about six o'clock, before Jerry was awake, his phone began ringing. It rang about three times before he answered it. "This better be good, Mother Fucker!"

"Would you like for me to call back next week?"

Recognizing Big Head's voice, Jerry changed his tone by saying, "If I knew it was you, I'd have baked a cake, my friend."

"Save it, Jerry. Just wake up because we're in luck. I got some action on what we talked about."

"Good, good. I knew I could count on you, ole buddy."

"You see, when the Big Head say's he's going to do something, he does it."

"Save it. Now I can see why they call you, Big Head."

Big Head laughed and said, "Anyway, can you have this person at the Las Vegas Zoo parking lot today at three o'clock?"

"Yeah, sure."

"If I'm not there yet, just wait for me. I won't be long. I wouldn't miss this for nothing. I'll explain everything then."

"Okay, be talkin to ya, eh."

* * * *

Martha, Herby's wife, shook him as he lay asleep on the couch. "Honey . . ."

"Huh . . . yeah?"

"Telephone."

"Okay," Herby grumbled as he got up and stretched. He then ambled over to the phone with a yawn before saying, "Hello."

"Jim, this is Jerry. Would you please meet me at the bar on the corner of 25th and Eastern at two thirty today?"

When he got out of his car at the specified location, he heard Jerry yell, "Over here, Jim!"

Herby locked his car and walked over to where Jerry sat in his car. "Hop in, we're going for a little ride if you don't mind." On their way out of town on the Tonapah Highway, they were both silent. Jerry's radio was playing Johnny Cash' *I Walk the Line*, which seemed to keep Herby entertained. When they pulled into the parking lot of the Las Vegas Zoo, they parked about three spaces from Big Heads car. When Jerry got out of his car, he said to Herby, "Sit tight, kid, I'll be right back." Then Jerry went over and got into the car with Big Head and asked, "What now, boss?"

"Okay, here it is. The mark is going to be hit in the zoo about three-thirty."

"Good."

"Take the kid into the zoo and start walking around with him," said Big Head, and then he explained everything that was planned.

"Is that it?" asked Jerry.

"Yep."

"Okay then, I'll be on my way, be talkin to ya, eh." Jerry returned to his car and got Herby, then they went into the zoo.

They spent about twenty minutes walking around until it was time. They came to the designated bench and sat down.

"Jim, at five o'clock it'll be time for you to go home. I'm telling you this just in case we get separated. At that time, you'll have no memory of what happened here today." A few minutes later, when Jerry spotted the bright red dress and the mark approaching, he asked: "Jim, would you like something to eat or drink?"

"No thanks."

"I do," replied Jerry, trying not to appear conspicuous or hurried. "I'll be right back then, sit tight." Jerry walked toward the concession stand. Big Head got his attention and waved him over. As Jerry was approaching, Big Head pointed and said, "Look, he can't see us, but we can see him."

"Perfect, and it's about to happen right now. Wow, the timing couldn't have been better. Where's the sniper at?"

Big Head showed him. It was only a matter of seconds now. They watched the sniper take aim, and they could tell that Herby was watching what was about to happen. Suddenly, a shot rang out; alarming everybody in the area. The woman in the red mini-skirt started screaming, as she stood over the slain man with her hands to her face in horror. Her walking partner lay on the sidewalk with his face blown off. Pandemonium! People screaming and scrambling everywhere. A crowd was gathering around the obviously dead man. Security guards were running toward the crowd blowing whistles. The P.A. system blaring instructions in a futile attempt to calm the panic. Little kids yelling and asking questions. Many of the animals in the vicinity were going berserk.

Casually and without emotion, Herby got up and walked away as though nothing happened. After having observed the whole affair, one would think that he didn't even care.

* * * *

The cheaters have been cheated and the anthros continued living their lives in their parallel universes with no further harassment from anyone trying to manipulate them. If anything, they were the ones capable of manipulation, but because anthros being basically honest, they didn't abuse their gifts.